WHAT GOES AROUND...

Written by

Mick Woodhall

Cover photo ©2008 Mintina
ISBN 978-0-6152-1224-1

CHAPTER I

Danny hoped the deputy would turn on his blue lights. Not because he was in any particular hurry to get to the hospital, but because the back-seat of a patrol car was not the most comfortable place on earth. Then again, Danny knew it wasn't designed to be. At least he wasn't handcuffed this time. That's the worst. Danny knew that when you're cramped up in the back of a patrol car with your hands cuffed behind you, you were pretty much at the cop's mercy.

Danny knew this because Danny had been there. Fifteen years old he had been at the time. Arrested for vandalizing a television station of all things. But that was two years ago. This time was different. This time he was in control. This time it was his plan, and it was going perfectly, so far.

Still, just being back in a patrol car made Danny uneasy. He looked out through the window at the passing buildings.

"Finally!" he whispered, as they turned into St. Michael's hospital emergency room entrance. Danny desperately wanted out of the patrol car. It was bringing too many memories back. Memories Danny did not want, and definitely did not need right now. He had to keep focused. He wasn't through this yet.

One good thing, he thought, at least his nose had stopped bleeding. It still hurt like hell though, and it had started to swell up across the bridge. He noticed the last part by leaning forward and looking at himself in the police car's rear view mirror. Danny hoped that he hadn't broken it. *She* hadn't broken it.

"Stay in character," he muttered under his breath. "Don't blow it now!"

As the deputy slowed into a spot marked for emergency vehicles only, Danny wondered just how his mom was doing at this moment.

"What the hell just happened here?!" Nick asked his wife after the deputy left with Danny. "I knew he had problems, hell, we both knew," Nick shook his head in disbelief, "but to go and do this? For what?!" Nick began to pace the floor in front of Pam.

"I don't know, Honey." Pam Roanik was crying, "I've never laid a hand on him in his life! Why would he

4

tell those awful lies?"

Nick knew they were lies. No, he didn't see it happen, but he did know his wife, and Nick believed her when she said that she didn't hit her son. They had been having trouble out of Nick's stepson for a couple of years now. Ever since he vandalized the television station where Nick worked. Nick remembered that day very well. Pam, Sally, and he had just returned from parent night at Sally's school. Sally was Pam's daughter, and Danny's little sister. A joy to work with, her teacher had told them. Nick was very proud of his step-daughter. They got such a good report on Sally that Nick had promised to make her his famous melted moon pie sundae when they got home. Sally would have to wait a bit longer than expected for her treat, though.

As Nick pulled their SUV up the driveway, they saw Danny sitting on the hood of his car. No, Danny couldn't drive yet. He didn't even have his license. Nick and Pam had given him a used Chrysler hatchback a year before his sixteenth birthday. That way, they figured, he would have a time to fix it up for when he got his license. It didn't work out that way though. Danny hadn't done so much with the car as even wash it since they gave it to him. That really surprised Nick. He remembered when he was a teen-ager and other than girls, there was nothing he dreamed more about than a car.

Not Danny though. All he did was sit on the hood. Sit on the hood and touch the windshield in that weird pattern of his. Index finger, tap-tap. Ring finger, tap-tap-tap. Pinkie, tap. Index finger, tap-tap-tap-tap. Over and over again. Never the middle finger though. If the middle finger accidentally touched something during this routine, Nick had noticed, Danny would shake his head, mumble under his breath, and start the whole thing all over again. Tap-tap. Apparently, his middle finger was sacred. To be used only towards his mother.

That routine was just what Danny was doing when his family came home that day. Nick and Pam looked at each other worriedly as they got out of the car. That was the first time the police had been out to their house.

It wasn't the first time, however, that Nick had seen Danny do his strange little finger dance, though. That was just one of the odd behaviors Nick had been noticing from his step-son over the years since they met. At first he thought it was just harmless teen-age weirdness. Like the time Nick came home early and found Danny down in the basement, masturbating up against the furnace. Nick was shocked at first. Not because he had caught the boy in the act of whacking-off or even Danny's chosen location for the act. Hell, Nick himself had spanked it in weirder places than beside a furnace in his youth. No, what shocked him was that even in the dark, Danny had to know that Nick

6

was there. A fact that didn't seem to embarrass, or even bother his stepson at all. He actually seemed to like it, Nick thought at the time. Only later did he dismiss that thought as ludicrous. What teen-age boy likes being caught masturbating? Nick remembered Danny just sitting there, staring at Nick with his fist wrapped around his penis, furiously pumping his erection. Or was he staring through me? Nick thought. Normal teen-age shit, with a twist. That was our Danny.

"Look, Honey," Nick found himself back in their living room at the sound of his wife's voice, "I'm sure protective services is on their way over here. The deputy said he would have to call them. He said it was required whenever a child is injured in domestic violence."

"What about when it's the child who does the abuse?" Nick asked her, shaking his head in disbelief.

This was all new to Nick. Thirty-five years old and he had never had any kids of his own. It was never a priority for him. He was the area's number two news anchor in a good sized western North Carolina market. His goal was to be number one, a position currently held by Gary Utley over at channel 9.

Nick was good at what he did, probably deserved to be number one, but his age cost him it every year. It was never actually said officially that that was the reason, but no one under forty had ever been number one in his or the surrounding markets, and Nick wanted to be the first.

"People just don't have as much faith in younger people giving them their news." Nick's boss had told him after one loss, "They want Walter Cronkite with them at the dinner hour, not Ritchie Cunningham."

Nick would not be put off. It was a challenge, and he was up for it. It was his top goal. That is, it was his top goal until that day in January almost four years ago when he first met Pam. She had come into the News 11 offices to meet a friend for lunch. The friend happened to be one of Nick's assistants, who, after introductions invited Nick to join them.

The three of them enjoyed crab salad and iced tea at the Seafood Sloop downtown. Pam and Nick practically dominated the conversation throughout lunch, apologizing to Nick's assistant, Tina, when they realized it. Pam was open about some things. Yes, she was from the area, but her parents grew up in Indiana and moved to the mountains before she and her brother were born. Somewhat more quiet on other issues, such as her recent divorce. Nick's reporter instincts sensed this was a delicate issue and not to push.

As they parted after lunch, Nick boldly asked her if she would like to have dinner with him sometime. He couldn't be more pleased that she said yes.

"How about Saturday night at your house?" Nick

asked. "I could cook, and I'd love to meet those wonderful kids you told me about." He gave her his best smile. He hadn't been kidding either. He truly loved to cook, it wasn't just some line he'd read from Playboy's list of what women want in a man.

Pam thought for a moment, this would be her first date since her divorce from Jeff, eight months earlier. She did find Nick both handsome and interesting. But was she ready? Pam looked at her friend Tina. She was smiling, her eyes said to go for it.

"All right." Pam said nervously, "7:30. My place. I'll have to feed Sally earlier though; five year olds' stomachs are on a different timetable than us bigger people."

Nick laughed, and told her that would be fine.

That was four years ago, and they've been together ever since.

"Nick, are you here? What are we going to do?" Pam brought him back to the present situation again.

Nick ran his hand through his wavy hair and looked at his wife. "We'll just tell them what really happened, Honey." He took her in his arms and wiped away a tear. "Tell me again, from the beginning."

"It's like I said," began Pam, "the kids and I had just finished watching your 6:00 broadcast. Well, Danny and I did."

9

Nick knew what she meant. Sally was like most nine year olds in that she didn't have much of an attention span for the news. Nick knew his stepdaughter loved him, but he also knew that he would have to take a distant second to Sponge-Bob Square-Pants when it came to his broadcasts.

"Go on, dear." Nick told her.

"Well, just as Seinfeld came on, Danny stood up and said he was sick of this shit, and was going to fix things." Pam was crying again.

Nick went to the bathroom and brought back a fresh box of tissues for her. Pam took them and continued. "Then he got a strange look in his eyes." She paused and wiped her nose. "That's when he started that finger thing."

"Tap-tap?" asked Nick, motioning in the air with his first and third fingers.

"Yes and when I grabbed his hand and told him to calm down, that we could talk about it, well, that's when he hit me."

Nick looked again at the blood that had dried on his wife's lip. How he wanted to kill the little bastard at that moment. Nick had never hit a woman in his life, and the thought of anyone putting their hands on his wife sickened him. How could a child want to do that to his own mother? Nick was choking up too.

"That's when he lost it," she sighed, "he flipped

10

over the coffee table and picked up the vase your mother

sent us. You know, the one made of gun metal that looks

like Barbara Eden's bottle on 'I Dream of Jeannie.' Then

I...I couldn't believe it. Nick, he smashed himself in the

nose with it and started screaming, 'You hit me! Why did

you hit me?'"

Nick put his arm around his shaking wife. "That's

when I came in," Nick said, "I saw him grab the phone and

lock himself in his room. The next thing I know, the police

are here and he was putting on one hell of a show."

"What's happened to him, Nick? What did I do

wrong?"

"You didn't do anything wrong, Honey." Nick was

sitting on the couch facing her now. He put his hands on

her shoulders, consoling her as he spoke. "We knew

something was wrong with him, even Dr. Williamson said

so."

Dr. Williamson was the psychiatrist that Danny had

to go to as part of the plea agreement they made when he

went to court for the vandalism. That, and thirty-six hours

of community service, plus cleaning his graffiti off the

television station walls.

Danny would rarely talk to the doctor. He said he

was ordered to come, not to participate. Every once in a

while he would come in different, though, ready to talk.

Mostly about his dad, and for a while about his girlfriend.

Dr. Williamson had also seen the tapping. He told Pam and Nick that he suspected that Danny had obsessive compulsive disorder. O.C.D. They would have to do some tests. Tests that would require Danny's cooperation.

That was the problem. They talked to Danny together; explaining how the tests could help properly diagnose him, help him have a normal life. Through the whole conversation the three adults noticed Danny's fingers tapping out the now familiar pattern on the arm of the black leather chair he sat in. When they had finished talking, Danny looked at them and said he wasn't the one with the problem, and that if they wanted to do any testing on anyone it should be on his mother. When Dr. Williamson asked him why he thought that, Danny just laughed and walked out of the room.

Back in their living room, still trying to make heads or tails out of what happened, Nick and Pam's breathing stopped when they saw the headlights turn into their driveway. Pam had been right; the investigators from the Department of Social Services were on their porch.

Nick answered the door while his wife sat on the couch, nervously touching the spot of dried blood on her lip.

"Mr. Roanik?" said the tall, well dressed woman in front. "I'm Ann Randall, from the Department of Social Services, and this is my co-worker, Patty Strickend."

Her "co-worker", Nick later realized, was no more than a social worker in training. Twenty-four years old, if she was a day.

"May we come in?" asked Ms. Randall. Without really waiting for a response, she brushed past Nick with her trainee in tow like a lost puppy. Already Nick didn't like her. She reminded him of that nosy neighbor that was always better than everyone else on that old Michael Landon show. What was it? Oh, yeah, Little House on the prairie. Only this wasn't a television show, and here Laura Ingalls wasn't a sweet little girl who chased frogs.

No sir, here Laura was a teen-age boy who masturbates against furnaces and hits his mother. Tap-tap-tap.

"Can I get you something to drink? Coffee, lemonade, a martini?" This was Pam's little attempt at a joke. She had a great sense of humor, but not always the best timing.

At her remark, social worker Ann Randall sniffed, "We at the department do not drink alcoholic beverages while on duty."

Now put away that frog and get on with your chores, Laura! Nick thought. He could picture the character, but for the life of him couldn't remember her name. All the while, Patty, whom Pam later told Nick reminded her of a social worker groupie, just sat there and stared at her boss with a kind of glassy eyed amazement.

"We've just come from the hospital where we talked to your son, Danny, Mrs. Roanik, and he told us that you punched him in the nose. What can you add to that?" Ann Randall glared over her glasses at Pam and Nick, while her faithful puppy took notes.

"I'll tell you what we can add," stressed Nick sarcastically, "How about the truth? Danny went berserk and hit himself in the nose with a vase and…"

Ms. Randall didn't let him finish. "You expect us to believe that poor boy did this to himself, Mr. Roanik? I'm appalled!" She pulled a stack of Polaroid photographs from a pocket in her briefcase, and tossed them onto the coffee table in front of Pam and Nick.

Nick had put the table back upright and cleaned up the mess before the police came and Danny tried for his Oscar. The pictures lying in front of them were all of Danny. More specifically Danny's nose, which had swollen considerably since Pam had last seen it.

Ann saw that this standard D.S.S. tactic had achieved the desired effect and continued. "Would you please show us this vase, Mr. Roanik?" She purposely left out the pictures so Pam would have to continue to look at them.

Before Nick could move he realized, in all the time since he'd gotten home he hadn't once seen the vase,

14

hadn't even asked his wife about it. He had even cleaned up the mess himself, putting back every little knick-knack, but no, the vase hadn't been there. He looked down at the table where they normally kept the vase, but in its place were the pictures of Danny's nose. He looked up at the social worker and noticed that she looked even more like Michael Landon's snooty neighbor than before. She was looking at him with that 'sure there's a vase' look.

"Well, Mr. Roanik?" She stared.

"Pam, what happened to the vase after he hit himself with it?" Nick asked his wife.

"I, I don't know! I was just so shocked that he would do such a thing, that I didn't notice what he did with it afterwards!" Pam's eyes were desperate.

Nick looked from his wife to Ann, and back to his wife again. "Well, look at her lip!" He pointed towards Pam, "Can't you see that he hit her?"

"Come now, Mr. Roanik. First the disappearing vase," Ann was positively loving this now. Laura Ingalls meets Perry Mason, "now you expect us to believe that poor boy hit his own mother? For all we know at this point, you could have hit them both."

Nick was floored. The trump card. He couldn't believe what he was hearing. "I think you need to leave!" Nick told them. As he opened the front door to show he wasn't kidding, Deputy Conner was about to ring the bell.

It was the same deputy that had been out earlier. The one that took Danny to the hospital.

"May I come in, sir?" said the young deputy.

"Certainly, officer," came Nick's reply.

"Hello again, ladies, Mrs. Roanik." The deputy nodded at each of them in turn. "I've taken Danny to the safe house as you requested when we met at St. Michael's, Ma'am." This was to Ms. Randall alone.

"What kind of game are you people playing?" demanded Nick. "I had better get some answers, right now!"

Pam shot him a look to tell him to calm down, but she knew it was no good. Her husband was the most easy going man she knew, but on the few occasions she'd seen him angry, she knew he didn't back down. She glanced over towards the social workers to see their reaction to Nick's outburst. Ann Randall's side-kick was writing furiously in her notebook, totally oblivious to the slight string of spittle hanging from the corner of her mouth. Pam looked on in disgust as it turned into kind of a spit bubble, then it popped and started it's journey down the woman's chin. Pam had seen enough. She turned to the leader as Ann stood up to speak.

"Mr. Roanik, Danny said his mother hit him; you say he hit himself with some vase. A vase you can't seem to produce. All of this makes us suspicious." Ann had the

16

whole rooms' attention. "The Department has done extensive studies in homes where step-parents play a vital role in a child's development and up-bringing."

"Are you suggesting…" stammered Nick as he stormed towards the woman.

Deputy Conner stepped in between them. "Relax, Mr. Roanik."

Nick hadn't noticed his hands clenched into fists until that moment. He relaxed and sat back down next to his wife. Pam put her hand on his knee. Nick covered her hand with his and looked at her. This was killing her, he thought. She seemed to have aged five years since this morning. Nick had a right to be mad. What gave these people the right to come into their home and make accusations like this? Was there some little read section of the United States Constitution that says 'this does not apply to The Department of Social Services?' He glared at Ann Randall with contempt.

"As I was saying," continued Ms. Randall, "children who are abused have a tendency to cling to their abuser, and sometimes even shun the other parent. In this case, Danny knows that his mother loves him and would never hurt him; she's protected him his whole life. Yet, he was very adamant that it was her that hit him, not you. He mentioned several times how much he loves you and that when you say he's bad and get angry at him that means you

17

love him. All the things he told us are clues, Mr. Roanik, clues social workers look for to filter out the truth in abuse cases."

Nick felt sick. The kind of sick you get when a cop is behind you on the road and you're not sure what the speed limit is.

"Look!" Pam stood up. "My husband is not an abuser. Danny needs help, not cookie cutter analyzing. I can't believe you're actually feeding us this shit. Do you have any actual training, Ms. Randall? Have you been to college, or is this veterinary social work you studied?" Pam couldn't remember the last time she'd been this angry.

"You fit the classic profile of an abused wife as well, Mrs. Roanik," continued Ann, "but you have nothing to worry about now. He won't be able to hurt your family again. Officer?"

"No, you idiot!" Pam yelled at Ann. "You need to take your damn studies and shove them up your bureaucratic ass! My husband wouldn't hurt a fly!"

Nick was feeling dizzy, he barely heard the deputy reading him his rights. He later found out that when it comes to D.S.S., you don't have any. None of this really hit home to Nick, that is until he heard the click of the handcuffs on his wrists. He had been handcuffed only once before in his life, after a stupid fraternity stunt back in college, and he didn't like it now anymore then he did then.

"You people are fucking idiots!" Pam picked up the photos of Danny and threw them at Ann Randall. "He's the problem, not Nick! What's wrong with you? Hell, your partner is sitting over here drooling on herself, and you think you're qualified to judge us? She probably isn't even house broken!"

Patty Strickend finally became aware, and wiped her mouth as everyone watched, her face red with embarrassment. Nick thought it would be a pretty comical moment if he hadn't been so scared.

"Let my husband go!" Pam was in Deputy Conner's face now. "I'm not pressing any charges. He didn't hit anyone!"

"That's for the Judge to decide, Mrs. Roanik," Ann seemed practically orgasmic now, "but in the event of domestic violence, the parties are to be separated, and the suspect incarcerated. That's the law in this state. Believe me Mrs. Roanik, it is for your protection." Ann Randall paused to catch her breath. "In the matter of Danny, however, since he is a minor, the Department has no other option than to take temporary custody of him. The Department also not only has the right, but also the obligation, to file the charges of abuse and neglect ourselves. Based on our findings here, as well as your refusal to co-operate, we have no other choice than to do just that. I think we're finished with Mr. Roanik at this time, deputy. You may take him."

Pam and Nick stared at each other in shock.

"Yes Ma'am. Let's go, Sir." Deputy Conner took Nick's arm.

She probably practices that speech in front of her mirror every morning with an applause tape playing in the background, thought Nick while glaring at what he now thought of as a social worthless. "Call Ted, Honey, and don't worry, we'll get through this garbage," Nick told Pam as he leaned forward to give her an awkward kiss.

With his hands cuffed behind him, this act made Nick feel like one of those plastic birds with the red liquid inside that bobs up and down over a glass of water, giving the appearance that he's drinking from it. Nick's father had owned one when Nick was a kid and as a boy he thought it was the coolest thing until he finally realized that the bird wasn't really drinking the water. It was just an illusion. First lesson in life Nicky-boy, don't always believe what you see.

As he straightened back up to leave he gave Ann Randall one last glare, and it hit him. Mrs. Olsen! That was that snooty know-it-all's name on that show! That's who you are Ms. Randall, Nick thought as the deputy took him out to his cruiser, and just like the show, you too will be canceled.

Pam knew she had to call Ted. Ted Anders was

their lawyer. Well, not really. Nick and Pam aren't the kind of people who need a lawyer on a regular basis, but Ted was their friend, and it just so happened he was also a lawyer.

"Is there any other aspect of my family's life that you want to screw up, Ms. Randall? Because if you're done, please take your drooling groupie and get the hell out of my house." Pam seethed.

"Well," smiled Mrs. Olsen. (I'm not through with you yet, Laura Ingalls!) "There is the matter of the other child currently residing here. Sally Nelson, I believe her name is," Ann said while studying some notes. "Where is she, Mrs. Roanik?"

The doctor said it wasn't broken, just bruised some, back in shape in no time. Just keep ice on it. Danny gingerly touched his nose and thought about that. Good, no permanent scars. He had wondered if he might have hit it too hard. Whoops! *She* might have hit it too hard. Don't fuck it up now.

Danny turned from the window of the second floor room that the good folks at the New Hope runaway shelter had assigned to him. He took stock in his surroundings. Next to the bed sat a table. Carvings of the names of previous tenants covered most of the top and legs. Yeah, that's just what Danny wanted, a permanent reminder that he had spent any time in this shithole. 'John Jessup was here', Danny read off one leg. How proud he must be, Danny thought.

An old yellow lamp with a smoke stained shade sat on a dingy doily at the center of the table. Danny reached down and turned the switch. A dull glow illuminated that side of the room.

There was a metal chest of drawers that had most of its blue paint peeled or scraped off of it against the far wall. Apparently John Jessup or one of the other table authors had a lot of free time up here. Danny had no intention of staying that long. Other than that there was just the bed in the room. Danny walked over and sat on it. The loud creak of the springs as he settled in let Danny know that the mattress had seen better days. It's probably the same sorry mattress that Edward Norton used in the movie Fight Club, he thought. It was lumpy, too. He pulled back the blanket and crisp white sheet to reveal just what he had suspected. Piss and cum stains covered the mattress. How the hell could anyone get a hard on here, let alone jack-off? He put the sheet and blanket back in their place and lay down, staring at the ceiling. Oh well, he smiled, at least it's better than where good old Nick the dick would be sleeping tonight.

Danny's father would be pleased. He hadn't seen his dad in a while, but they talked a lot on the phone.

Whenever his mom and Nick weren't around, that is.

Danny's mother had divorced his dad, Jeff Nelson, about four years earlier amid allegations of his dad practicing necraphila at his funeral home. Danny didn't know what exactly that word meant at the time, but he overheard his mom on the phone once telling her nosy friend Betty that, "Jeff had been a dead fuck for years, but I didn't think he fucked the dead." Danny remembered his mother laughing at the cleverness of her statement, and at his father.

The police didn't have enough evidence for the district attorney to prosecute Jeff, so the charges were dropped. It was never proven and his dad was set free, but Danny's mother couldn't take the pressure. Everyone knew about it. She lost all of her friends, except Betty. The two of them had been friends since high school and it would take a little more than some corpse-a-lingus to divide them.

Just how did everyone know about Jeff Nelson's situation? Why, Channel 11 ace reporter, Nick Roanik, that's how. Danny didn't know Nick personally at that time.

On that fateful day, Danny had been at home, channel surfing out of boredom. He had given up on MTV, and flipped around the dial when he came to channel 11. He stopped there because he saw his dad. His dad, handcuffed, walking between two deputies with this idiot holding a microphone that he kept shoving in Jeff Nelson's face, asking dumbass questions like "Did you have sex with the late Mrs. Tabbing?"

That was all it took. Even though the charges were never proven and the case dropped, Jeff lost everything. After all, true or not, would you take your dearly departed sister, daughter, mother or wife to a funeral home that came to be known as 'you slay'em, I'll lay'em'?

Danny's mom still let Danny and Sally visit their dad for a little while after the divorce. That was until Sally came home one Sunday evening after a weekend visit with a new word to share. Whore. "Daddy told us that's what you are," she told her mother, smiling. Sally didn't know what the word meant, but boy was Pam pissed. She called Jeff that night after the kids went to bed and let him have it. Sally hadn't been back since. Danny however, would continue to beg and pressure his mother to see Jeff, and sometimes she would reach her limit and give in.

What conversations Danny and his dad would have when they were together. They would sit in Jeff's little one bedroom trailer and talk for hours. Jeff had to move into the trailer after the bank took the house. After all, landscaping and odd jobs don't pay as well as owning your own funeral parlor.

They'd sit together on Jeff's worn couch and he would tell Danny how it was Nick who broke up their family. Between gulps of Jeff's now ever present can of beer, he would talk about how that whore Pam had cheated on him with Nick for years while they were married. How she, on the few occasions that she would allow Jeff inside her, would only do it when the news was on. So she could watch that bastard during their private moments.

Jeff would then tell Danny how Nick and Pam set him up to ruin him before they ran off together. How the Nelsons would still be a family if it weren't for that bastard Nick.

Of course none of this was true. Pam didn't even know Nick at that time, but Jeff was very convincing. Danny had no reason to think that his poor father would lie to him.

A few beers later and Jeff's whole attitude would change. His eyes half shut and his words so thick that Danny really had to strain to understand him, Jeff would mumble that he still loved Pam. That he would take her back and even forgive her for being a whore. Jeff would say that Pam wanted to be with him again but she's afraid of Nick. Usually it was shortly after this part that Danny stopped understanding his dad. His words became no more than half formed mumbles sprinkled between swearing and snores. Danny would grab the can of beer from his passed out dad's hand just before it slipped out of his relaxing grip and onto the stained carpet. He must sleep like this a lot,

Danny would think, looking at the stains from when nobody was there to catch the can before it fell.

Danny didn't remember his dad drinking so much when they all lived together. He would look around the run down trailer and wonder how his mom could have done this to him. He didn't understand how his father could even think of wanting that whore back after what she did. That is, Danny didn't understand it back then. Before Jane.

When he was a sophomore in high school, Danny had been getting serious with this cute little freshman by the name of Jane Conyers. She had long brown hair and big full lips. Lips that had Danny running to the furnace even before they had gotten together. It took him a month to work up the nerve to talk to her. He needn't have worried though, she later told him. She had been hoping he would say hi or something for almost the same amount of time. Jane was new at Adam's High School and very shy. She had noticed right away that Danny was different than the other boys at the school. He didn't follow the crowd. She liked that about him.

Besides, her father had warned her when they moved there from New York that she had better not even think about bringing home some backwoods redneck boy with flakes of chewing tobacco in what's left of his teeth.

Once Danny broke the ice, the two were inseparable. They talked about everything together.

Everything except the things his father told him. Danny wanted to, more than once. Especially when Jane would tell him how great it must be to have a somewhat famous person like Nick Roanik as a step-dad. Danny would always cringe at that. Yeah, and a whore for a mother, Danny would think. A regular Brady fucking bunch.

Danny lay on his bed at the New Hope runaway shelter and sighed as the memories came flooding back in his mind. He thought about the first time she let him touch her breasts, small and firm. They were the first ones he had ever felt. It had taken him three tries while they were making out on the couch in his basement one night before she stopped pushing his hand away. She had wanted it all along, Danny thought later that night while masturbating against the furnace.

For seven months they were together. Taking each others virginity just two weeks after he first touched her breasts. No doubt about it, Danny was in love. He also had a teenager's cockiness that let him believe that she loved him back, although neither of them ever said it.

Then came that Tuesday in the fall of his junior year. Danny had gotten himself another one of Mr. Farly's famous after school detentions. Mr. Farly handed out detention slips like communion wafers at a catholic church. Most of them going to Danny. He didn't much like Danny. That was OK. Danny didn't much like Mr. Farly. Besides,

the teacher wouldn't be a problem to Danny much longer.
Six months from that day Mr. Arnold Farly was fired from
his history teaching position at Adams High when a pile of
child porn pictures were found in his desk. Upon further
investigation, the principal found that Mr. Farly's computer
access code was being used to access child porn on the
school's computer.

Danny watched the news that night to see good ol'
Nick, in his blue sport coat, telling the good folks of
western N.C. about the sick, perverted teacher at the local
high school. The video footage showed Mr. Farly being
hauled away by Sheriff's deputies while yelling something
about not knowing how those disgusting pictures got in his
desk to a disbelieving crowd of parents and faculty. Danny
just smiled. There sure are some disturbed people in this
world, he thought.

Back on that particular Tuesday, before Mr. Farly's
fall from grace, Danny was sitting at a desk in room A-16.
The detention room. He was doodling on his binder while
trying to decide where to take Jane that evening. There was
a movie at the multiplex he'd wanted to see. The new one
with Bruce Willis. Danny liked Bruce Willis movies. Even
the one where he was a singing cat burglar. The critics
panned that one. Fuck the critics. Weren't they the same
dumbasses who said that The Love Boat was quality
television?

About that time, Danny looked out the window towards the football field. It was a beautiful September day, all right. Still enough like summer to make you hate school. As he was thinking this, someone caught the corner of his eye over by the concession stand. It was closed now, but would be ready for business that weekend when Adam's Rockets took on the Jefferson Titans.

What caught Danny's eye that day would hold his interest more than any stupid football game. It was Jane, leaning against the corner of the little concession shack with her arms around some guy. A guy that was obviously not him.

Turn around you cocksucker! Let me see who you are! fumed Danny as he got up from his desk and walked over to the window for a closer look.

"Sit back down, Danny! You still have twenty minutes left!" It was Mrs. Raburn. Algebra. She pulled detention duty that week.

She would have to say it three more times before Danny heard her, but by then he had seen enough. He had seen his girlfriend (WHORE!) kissing Eddie Jenkins full on the mouth. Danny had suspected it was the new senior at school. After all, how many kids here have a flat top hair cut? Danny wasn't totally sure though until they turned and started walking towards the parking lot with their arms around each other.

He felt sick as he returned to his desk. Sick and pissed. That whore! Danny never called her again, but now he understood what his father meant. He loved Jane and he would forgive her for being a whore when she came crawling back to him. But that never happened. Not even weeks later when the police took Eddie Jenkins to jail for possession of marijuana.

Pretty stupid! thought Danny that day. Danny sat behind Eddie in Health class, so he saw it happen. What kind of idiot brings an ounce of dope to school in his backpack? The exact same backpack that he slung over the back of his chair everyday, in a way that caused the metal clasp on the flap to constantly click against Danny's desk. Clicking out a melody that began to sound to Danny like 'your girlfriend's a whore and your mom's one even more,' over and over again. After awhile Danny found his own finger's repeatedly tapping out the same melody on his desk. Of course this was done unconsciously.

Yeah buddy, a backpack full of dope brought to class the same day Mrs. Swanson had already informed the students that the schools' DARE officer would be bringing in a drug sniffing dog for their yearly presentation and lecture. You should have seen the look on that dumbass Eddie's face when the dog went right up to his desk and sat down. It was almost as good a look as the surprised one he had on his face when the DARE officer pulled out the bag of pot and held it up in Eddie's face.

"I don't know how that got in there!" stammered Eddie as the cop read him his rights.

There seems to be a lot of that going around, Danny told himself while they led Eddie away. 'Your girlfriend's a whore and your mom's one even more' Danny unconsciously tapped over and over on his desk using only his first, third, and pinkie fingers. Never his middle one.

No, Danny and Jane were done. To him she was a whore. A whore that Danny still loved. Just like his dad still loved Pam. Sometimes it sickened him to refer to her as mom. After the Jane incident Danny felt even closer to Jeff Nelson. Dad. They understood each other.

Danny's thoughts took him so far away from the present situation that he almost fell asleep on the stained mattress, lost in his memories. Shaking his head free of the past, he bolted upright in the bed. There was something he had yet to do. A part of his plan he had almost forgotten about.

He swung his legs over the side of the bed and let his feet touch the hardwood floor. He hadn't even taken off his shoes yet. As he stood up, Danny stretched and popped his neck. He unconsciously touched his hurting nose again as he walked the length of the room and opened the door. Looking out in the darkened hallway, he suddenly realized how late it was. So much had happened in the five hours since Nick last read from his Teleprompter, trading bad jokes with his Channel 11 (reporting the facts. First!), co-anchor Kathy Skinner.

Danny doubted that they found the vase. He was pretty sure they didn't know about the loose floorboard in his bedroom closet. He himself had come across it by accident one day a while back and used the space under it to hide stuff that he didn't want anyone to find. Fuck books, letters from Jane, even a bag of pot one time. The vase fit perfectly, and he had plenty of time to stash it before the police showed up. Yes, it was still safely in its place. Otherwise, he was sure, he would have known about it.

Danny had made it across the hall and halfway down the stairs when the quiet night was broken by the faint sounds of the television coming from the community room. That's what the New Hope shelter's director, Mr. Johnston, had called it earlier as he gave Danny the grand tour. The community room. It looked more like the Salvation Army to Danny, what with all the mismatched, ratty furniture in there.

"Oh, this will never do!" He could hear his mother saying. Pam Roanik was the type of person who buys 'peach' toilet paper to match the peach shower curtain in the guest bathroom. The one with towels you look at, (peach), and towels you use (also peach). Yeah buddy,

32

What Goes Around   by Mick Woodhall

Danny thought, and they say *I'm* obsessive.

He paused when he reached the landing and looked around the corner towards the community room. The door was closed but he could see the light from the television flickering underneath. He imagined the evenings 'youth counselor', (guard-bitch), flopped out on the fake leather couch watching some late night talk show.

Mr. Johnston had explained the house rules when Danny arrived. Only two of them caught Danny's interest. Number 7: Do not practice self gratification while on the premises. Danny thought that they didn't enforce that one enough after he saw his mattress. Also rule number 12, 'All tenants will observe a 10:00 bedtime.' Since it was well past ten he had to be quiet.

He turned away from the community room and walked the other direction, towards the kitchen. The old linoleum was cracked and dingy and it made little popping sounds with each step Danny took. It wasn't loud enough to be heard by the guard-bitch, (youth counselor), but just to be on the safe side Danny slid his feet the rest of the way instead of walking. He'd come too far to have his plan ruined by some cheap flooring and a nosy social worker trainee. Ten seconds later he was at his destination.

Danny picked up the phone and wiped both the mouth and ear piece with a paper towel. As he put the phone to his ear he whispered the sequence of numbers that he had memorized months before as he pushed the coinciding buttons. When it started ringing he looked back over his shoulder to make sure he was still alone. He was.

"Channel 9 news, can I help you?" The voice on the other end repeated.

"Yes Ma'am," said Danny quietly, "Would you be interested in knowing the name of a certain news person who at this moment is sitting in jail for child abuse?"

CHAPTER II

"What did you say?" Pam couldn't believe what she was hearing.

"I said, we need to discuss what we're going to do about Sally Nelson, Mrs. Roanik, where is she?" Ms. Randall asked again.

"She's spending the night at a friend's house." Replied Pam. "What does she have to do with this anyway?"

"Well, Mrs. Roanik," Pam turned her attention to Patty, who by now had wiped her mouth and was trying to earn her pay, "Whenever there is an instance of a child being abused by his or her parent, especially with the force your husband hit Danny…"

"My husband did not hit Danny!" Pam interrupted with a stern coldness that rivaled that of Ann Randall's. "And if you persist on continuing with that accusation then I strongly suggest you learn, and use, the word 'allegedly' before I decide to sue your drooling ass for slander!"

Patty Strickend was stunned by the attack. She

looked over to her boss for help.

"Mrs. Roanik, it would be in everyone's best interest if we calmed down and handled this like adults." Ann began, "What Patty was trying to say is that in cases where one child in the family dynamic has, allegedly," she looked over at her now quiet assistant and winked, "been abused, we find it is best to remove all minors that could be at risk from the household." She opened her briefcase and took out some forms. "Now, since your husband is out of the household for the time being, and your daughter is at a friend's house, out of harms way for the night, I see no reason to disrupt her at this hour." She was writing on one of the forms as she spoke, "The Department suggests to you very strongly that you spend the remainder of the evening trying to come up with a family placement for Sally. We always try to go that route first if possible, Mrs. Roanik, with foster care as a last option."

"Family placement? Foster care? This is a child, you idiot, my child! You're supposedly worried about child safety and development? What the hell do you think yanking a well adjusted little girl out of her home is going to do to her?" Pam was beyond crying now.

"You should have thought about that before you let an abuser, sorry, 'alleged' abuser into your home." Ann stood up and handed Pam a form. "Have Sally at our office by 10:00 tomorrow morning or a warrant will be issued for you, at which point the Department will have to consider family placement no longer an option and will petition the court to put Sally into our custody. Have a good night, Mrs. Roanik. Come on Patty, let's go get some coffee. There's a great new place up the road from here."

Pam sat in her chair stunned. She could hear the two social workers talking and laughing as they walked to their car. She couldn't believe it. In less than two hours D.S.S. had destroyed her whole family and then went out for coffee as if they had just had their hair done. Pam felt sick. They can't be able to get away with this. She got up and walked down the hall and into the kitchen, grabbing a bottle of Southern Comfort from the pantry on the way. She had never been much of a drinker but she was shaking so bad she needed something to calm her nerves or she felt that she was going to lose it. She did anyway.

After pouring some of the liquid from bottle to glass, she slammed it back and swallowed hard.

"Oh, thank you for coming at this hour Ted. Hi Nora." For the first time in hours Pam seem relieved, "I didn't know what else to do."

"I'll start by making us all some coffee," said Nora after hugging her friend, "and let's put this away, it can't help matters." Nora picked up the now half empty bottle of liquor and gave her husband a concerned look as she put it back in the pantry.

"Yes, of course you're right. Thanks for the coffee. Ted, please sit down."

Ted closed the living room drapes and took a seat in the recliner. He took a pen and legal pad from his briefcase and looked up at Pam. "Let's start from the beginning, and tell me everything."

Pam sat on the end of the couch and took a deep breath before going into the story for the third time that night. She got through it pretty well, all things considered. She only got choked up twice. The first time while describing her husband's arrest, and then again while telling about D.S.S. wanting to remove Sally from their home. Pam's anger returned as she was telling them about how callous Ann Randall and Patty Strickend had been about it.

"How can they do that, Ted? Just come in someone's home and make accusations like that?" asked Pam while pouring a second cup of coffee for everyone. "It seemed to me that those people at D.S.S. had their minds made up about us before they even arrived!"

"Well, Pam, the system isn't perfect. In this case it's a down right joke, but I've dealt with D.S.S. on a number of other cases and their standard response is that they aren't there for the parents; they're there to help the child. Unfortunately, a lot of times they do more long term damage to the kids with the standard cookie-cutter way they handle cases like these." Ted paused and took a sip of coffee, glancing over his notes. "From what you told me, as well as what I know about you and Nick," Ted smiled warmly at Pam, "you have nothing to worry about concerning the abuse charge against Nick on you or Danny. The Department always feels the step-parent is at fault when these things happen. Having Nick arrested and taken out of here was just a quick fix to calm the situation down in their eyes."

Pam relaxed a little.

"When I leave here," continued Ted, "I'll go to the magistrate's office and see what we can do about getting bail set on Nick. Nora, will you stay with Pam until I get back?"

"It's already decided." Nora replied while patting Pam's knee. Pam covered Nora's hand with her own.

"Thank you so much." Pam sighed as Ted set his cup on the coffee table and got up to leave.

Ted put his notepad back in his case and walked over to where Pam was now standing. Putting his hands on her shoulders and looking into her puffy eyes he told her, "This is hard for you, I know, but you'll have to be strong. This could be a long road for you. D.S.S. isn't known for admitting they've made a mistake. They'll twist everything you two say or do to their advantage. Now, this part is very important," Ted hugged her and let go, still keeping eye contact, "do not, under any circumstances, talk to them or meet with them without me present. Also, as much as you don't like it, be nice to them. For Sally's sake."

Pam nodded her head, taking this all in. Be nice to them. Sure, Pam thought, for now. For Sally. When this was over however, she would have a thing or two to say to Ann Randall.

Ted kissed his wife and told them both good-bye. Then he left for the magistrate's office.

Nick sat on the concrete bench in the county jail's holding cell and hoped to God that Pam had been able to reach Ted. He looked around at his surroundings and was sure, more sure than he had ever been about anything, that he did not want to spend the night in this place.

The room was rectangular. About eight feet by twenty feet with a concrete bench coming out of the wall along both sides of the long part of the rectangle. No bars, just that extra thick glass with the wire criss-crossing through it that spanned one whole side above that wall's bench. There wasn't much of a view though, nothing but a hallway and wall as far as Nick could see. More concrete. There was the door they brought him in through at one end

40

of the cell, and at the other end there were two toilets. The strange thing about them was not that there were no dividers between the rest of the cell and the toilets. No, Nick thought, he'd seen that sort of thing at many a concert venue or sports arena. No, what he had never seen before was that the two toilets were on opposing walls, facing each other. That's just what Nick wanted. Company while he took a shit. And the company he would have tonight, assuming that he ended up having to use one of the community toilets, consisted of seven other guys in various states of consciousness. The worst of which being, Nick thought, the middle aged guy currently asleep on one of the toilets with his dirty jeans around his ankles. Passed out in the middle of a shit. Damn, how drunk can you get?

Two other guys, they looked to Nick like they were in their mid-twenties, sat at the other end of the cell with their arms around each other. The thinner one was asleep on the other one's shoulder. The kind of people who would actually enjoy the community toilet set up that the cell had, Nick told himself.

The guy asleep on the toilet suddenly let out a loud fart and started mumbling to himself. Nick was amused and amazed that even this didn't wake him.

Nick sighed and leaned back against the wall. He couldn't believe any of this was happening. He didn't even know how long he'd been there. They took his watch when he was being processed. Hell, the bastards even took his wedding band. That pissed Nick off most of all. That ring had not been off his hand since Pam put it on his finger on their wedding day. Everything he had was put in a manila envelope labeled Roanik, Nick P.

Another fart from the tidy bowl man. This time he did wake up. The man looked around confused for a second, then as his head cleared; a look of understanding came over his face. Understanding what, Nick wondered. That he was in jail or that he passed out on the toilet? The man stood up and pulled up his pants, didn't even bother to wipe his ass. Too much energy involved. Nick knew that he had seen more than he ever needed to when the man then laid down in front of the unflushed toilet and went back to sleep in a puddle of some other drunk's piss.

God, get me out of here! screamed Nick's brain.

A well dressed man snoring on the floor in the middle of the cell had now woken up. He looked at the two queers and then at Nick, taking stock over what's new since he fell asleep. He was now refreshed and felt like talking. He decided against the two lovers, who were now lying down almost on top of each other, sleeping on the bench in each others arms.

The man cleared his throat and got up on the bench directly across from Nick. "Man, I sure could use a cigarette," he Said to Nick.

Great, Nick thought without looking up. The last thing he wanted was a jail buddy. No, not true. The last thing he wanted was a jail romance, but a jail buddy was in the top five. Right up there with group showers and being in here long enough to need one of those toilets.

"Hell, maybe this would be a good time to quit." The man smiled at Nick. "You know," he said after a long, quiet pause, "for a guy that talks up a storm on the boob-tube every night, you sure don't have much to say."

At this, Nick looked up from the stain on the floor that he had been focusing on. Things just keep getting better, Nick thought.

"This isn't how or where I typically make acquaintances," Nick snarled.

"Well, I'll be!" chuckled the prisoner, noticing but choosing to ignore Nick's tone. "You aren't battery operated after all! Charlie Tibbens is the name." He held his hand out for Nick to shake. Even after it became obvious that Nick had no intention of receiving it, Charlie still kept it offered. "Must be your first time," he went on, "I guess this would be about my fifth. Hell, it's getting to be a routine thing in my line of work. Now don't be thinking I'm some kind of degenerate, 'cause I'm not. The people I watch are the degenerates. Well, not all of them, some are good people that got into bad situations, that's all. Go on, Nick, may I call you that? Shake it, I ain't got no

43

disease."

Nick finally shook the man's hand. If for no other reason than at least the man's babbling helped take his mind off his own troubles.

"The people you watch?" questioned Nick, "What is it that you do for a living Charlie? A peeping tom?"

Charlie let out a howl that would wake the dead. When he did, the guy by the toilet rolled over and mumbled something as he settled back in his puddle.

"You could say that, Nick. Actually, that is a big part of my job. I'm a private investigator. It's not as exciting as they make it look on TV though, if that's what you're thinking. I'm no Jim Rockford, that's for sure. No, it's mostly just husbands and wives that want me to follow their spouse around for a few days, for whatever reason."

"What got you in here?" Nick asked when Charlie finally stopped for a breath. "Did you peep through the wrong window and piss someone off?"

"No, actually this time it's on a personal level, Nick. I missed a couple of child support payments and this is my ex's way of reminding me. How about you?"

Nick wasn't all that comfortable telling what happened to a complete stranger. "Some bullshit between my stepson and D.S.S.," he mumbled.

"Ya belted him one and he reported you, eh buddy? That's happening more and more lately. How old is he?"

44

Charlie seemed interested.

"No, I didn't hit him. I wasn't even home when it happened. He hit himself and D.S.S. has this thing about step-parents. They've done studies, you know." Nick's bitterness was strong as he said this.

Charlie stared at him in disbelief. "Hit himself, you say? If you weren't there when it happened, who was? Your wife?" He leaned forward, intrigued.

"Yes. I got home shortly before the police arrived. Look, Charlie, no offense, but I'm not sure I should be talking to you about all this. I haven't even talked to my lawyer yet." Nick leaned his head back against the cool concrete wall and closed his eyes. He was getting one of those headaches of his.

Charlie disregarded this and pressed on. "So your wife told you that he hit himself? Did you say this is your stepson? I mean, your wife is his biological mother and you came along later?"

"Just what are you getting at?" Nick bolted upright, visibly irritated.

"Now calm down there pal, I'm not getting at anything. It's just, this sounds very familiar. A few years ago I had this case that…"

The lock clicked in the door and they turned to see who was going to be joining them. It was a deputy, "Roanik! Nick Roanik!" He read from is clipboard.

Nick looked at Charlie and stood up, "Yes Sir, I'm Nick Roanik."

The deputy looked across the room at him. A look, one that seemed to be searching, came across his face. The deputy knew Nick from somewhere, but couldn't place him. "Bail's been made. Come with me."

Nick started to leave when Charlie grabbed his arm. "Remember, Charlie Tibbens. Look me up. I think we should talk."

"Yeah, right, thanks. I'll do that." Nick gave him a look as he pulled away and started to work his way around the passed out drunks littering the floor. He had no intention of looking up Charlie Tibbens or any other aspect of his time there.

Nick walked through the door, and as the deputy closed it he heard a last wet fart from the man in the piss pool. A fitting good-bye from this shit hole, Nick told himself.

As they turned the corner at the end of the long corridor that opened up into the processing room, Nick could see Ted through the bullet proof glass that separated the prisoners from the rest of the world. Nick waved and followed the deputy to the counter. The deputy went behind the counter while Nick went to the other side and stood on the rubber feet that had been glued to the floor in front of each window. 'DO NOT LEAN ON THE COUNTER'

Nick read the sign on the ledge. The sign was written in both English and Spanish. We don't discriminate; we have a cell for everyone, thought Nick.

The deputy then started pulling items out of an envelope, calling out what each item was and how many, as he handed Nick back his possessions. One gold band. One watch, and so on. Nick couldn't help but be reminded of the scene from the beginning of the Blues Brothers movie. The part where John Belushi, as Jake Blues, was being released from prison and his envelope contained 'one used condom.'

The deputy looked up and glared at Nick. He hadn't realized that he had laughed out loud at this. "One ("used condom", Nick thought again) black onyx ring." The deputy finished his list. He set the envelope on the counter after handing out the final item. Nick then signed the form stating that every item he had upon arrival had been returned to him.

"Go through that door, your first appearance date is on this release form." Were the officer's final words as he handed Nick the papers. Nick put on his watch and looked at the time. 1:30 in the morning. What a night.

When he reached for the door, the guard buzzed it open from a button behind the counter. Ted stood up and walked over to his friend.

"Damn, you're ripe!" he said to Nick, wincing.

"What kind of cologne is that? Essence of convict?" Ted laughed.

"Brute, by Men-on-men, it's a prison favorite." Nick's smile was strained. "Damn, it's good to be out of there. Thanks for helping, Ted. I hate to sound rude, but can we get the hell out of here? Even just standing in the lobby makes me uneasy now. Kind of the underlying fear that they'll realize they made some kind of mistake and run out here to lock me back up. Stupid, huh?"

"I can't say if it's stupid or not, I've never been locked up. I can, however, get you home to your lovely wife. She's worried sick over all of this."

"Her and me both," Nick sighed.

The two men walked in silence to Ted's car. Suddenly it was as if night turned to day. Nick turned around, shielding his eyes from the glare.

"Is it true that you beat up your wife and son, Mr. Roanik?" Channel 9 news reporter, Phil Wesson, asked into his microphone before thrusting it into Nick's face.

Shit, this is all I need, thought Nick. Do I look that stupid when I'm on that side of the story? He wondered.

"No comment." Ted kept repeating to each of their questions as he hurried Nick into the passenger seat.

"Will you be representing him at his hearing?" They were asking Ted as he got into the drivers' side.

"No comment." Ted shut the door and put the key

48

into the ignition. "Sorry," he looked at his friend, "they weren't here when I arrived. If I had known, we would have left through a side door."

"They would have had those exits covered, too." Nick said absently. "Let's just get home. If they're here, then they are probably bothering the hell out of Pam and our neighbors by now. Hell, that's what I would be doing if I were them. How'd they find out so fast, Ted?"

"I don't know, but don't worry, I'll find out." Ted answered with determination as they made a right turn out of the parking lot and onto College Street.

When they approached the turn for Londonderry road, where the Roaniks had lived in peace for years, Ted stopped the car.

"Looks like you were right, Nick. Look at them; they're like vultures." Ted looked over at Nick and suddenly felt stupid. "Sorry, I didn't mean any…"

"That's all right. I guess it's time I learned how the other side felt about us reporters. Right now a good car crash or robbery would be nice. Hell, even a late night dog show. Anything to turn their attention away from us. I hate to say things like that, but I can only imagine what Pam is going through right now. Even without the media circus tearing up our lawn," Nick told his friend.

Ted thought for a moment. "Tell you what, why don't the two of you bed down at our house tonight? It will give us time to work out our game plan. Besides, you'll never get any rest with that reporter rodeo going on over there."

"How can we get Pam? As soon as she walks out the door, they'll be all over her. Then they'll just follow us. Move the rodeo, as you call it, to your yard."

Ted laughed and pulled out his cell phone. "You news hounds think you're so smart. Got every angle covered, eh? Watch this." Ted dialed Nick's house and after two rings Pam picked up.

"Ted? Thank God for caller I.D.! Is Nick with you? Is he all right? The news people are all over our front yard. They've been calling all night!"

"Calm down, Pam." Ted reassured her, "Nick's here and he's fine. Could use a shower, though." He winked at his friend. "We're around the corner. We see all the reporters. Look, here's what I want you to do. Leave the house just as it is. Don't turn any of the lights off. You and Nora slip out the back door. They won't be back there. Wouldn't dare risk the lawsuit. Besides, you guys keep the fence locked, right?"

Pam was listening, "Right! I get it. We'll cut through our backyard, hop the fence over to the Sampson's, and meet you on Buckeye Street! Great idea, Ted! These idiots will think we're still here and watch our house all night. Our own personal security system. Serves them right." Pam laughed.

"Good girl. Now get a few things for Nick, Sally, and yourself. This might not blow over in just one night." Ted told her. "Now get going. Pretend you two are teenagers sneaking out past curfew."

They both laughed and hung up. Nick looked at Ted with admiration. "When I get back to work I'm going to remember that trick, you know."

"That's OK. We've got a lot more. Let's get over to Buckeye Street and pick up our dates, Junior."

Nick was starting to feel better.

It seemed to them that it took forever for Pam and Nora to get out to the car. Nick was just about to go after them when he saw Pam come out of the darkness beside the Sampson's split level. He ran over and hugged his wife as hard as he could. Nora brought their suitcase to the trunk and handed it to her husband before kissing him. Ted put it inside, and put his arm around Nora as she watched their friends kiss like they haven't seen each other for years. They both smiled when Pam pulled back and told Nick that he had a date with a bar of soap, and that she was going to burn the clothes that he had on. Then she rested her head on his chest with the security of his strong, if overly pungent, arms around her.

After a minute of this, Nora reminded them that the reporters could circle the block. The four of them looked up the street and quietly got into the car for the drive to the

Anders' home.

"You know what, Honey," began Pam coyly, "I'm

beginning to hate reporters."

They all laughed at that. Even number two

newscaster, Nick Roanik.

After a restless night which consisted of a lot of

coffee and planning, and very little sleep, the Roaniks and

Anders had worked out the details of what to do about

Sally. Danny was another matter all together, but one thing

at a time.

Ted had an old friend from law school who now sat

on the bench. Ted, Nick, and Pam went to his office at 8

o'clock the morning that they were due at D.S.S. to see

what he could do. They were lucky that Judge Sawyer

remembered how well his friend Ted had helped him get

through some tough parts back in school, and was more

than happy to return the favor by helping them out.

What the plan was, Ted explained to him after

introductions were made, was that Pam and Nick would

sign over temporary custody of Sally to the Anders which

would prevent D.S.S. from being able to touch her. Of

course, Ted knew that he couldn't officially word it that

way, but this was a friendly meeting.

Judge Sawyer, after carefully listening to their plan,

thought for a moment before bringing up a few issues for

Ted to clarify. The first being that Nick was only Sally's step-father, what of the real father? Why wasn't he part of the situation?

Pam and Nick had expected this, and worked with their lawyer on how to handle it. It seems, Ted had told them, that there is a little known law on the state books that says if a non-custodial parent has made no contact with said child for a period of twelve consecutive months, that parent then forfeits all rights to said child. When they heard this from him, Pam let out a sigh of relief. Jeff Nelson has continued to talk with Danny, but more than a year had past since the 'whore' incident, the last time Sally had seen her father. First the birthday cards stopped, then the Christmas gifts, and finally the child support. It was as if Jeff had just written his daughter off like some bad debt, they told the judge.

It was hard on Sally at first. She remembered all the bad things her father had told her about Nick. How it was wrong for her to love him, that Nick really didn't like her. The kind of things that can scar a child, but as time went on; she saw that Nick really did care for her. He was there when she needed him. So over time they built a close loving bond that not even her father could destroy.

Judge Sawyer nodded. "Well, obviously that does leave Danny out of the equation, but I think we could do something about Sally." He looked thoughtfully at Pam, "I know it's none of my business, but I can't help but ask. When the child support stopped coming, why didn't you do something? Just because your ex-husband stopped being a part of your daughter's life, doesn't excuse him from his financial responsibilities."

Pam looked at Nick and held his hand tighter. "When it happened, it was heartbreaking seeing what it did to Sally. We talked about it and felt that if we pushed the child support issue then we might be ordered to make Sally go back over there. That was a risk that we just couldn't take. What little bit he was sending each week wasn't worth my," she squeezed Nick's hand, "our daughter's well being."

The Judge nodded, satisfied with the explanation. Here was a mother deeply protective of her children. He turned back to Ted. "D.S.S. can still fight the temporary custody order. I'm sure you're prepared for that. You've dealt with them before. Challenging them is like jumping into a snake pit. They love to flaunt their power, and when it's taken from them they don't deal with it very well."

"Yes, I know. We're prepared for that." Ted looked towards his friends to show his confidence.

"All right then, it's done." Judge Sawyer signed the order and gave a copy to Ted and put one in his out box for the clerk to file. "Good luck to you both, Mr. And Mrs. Roanik," he said as they all stood up to shake hands. "I

hope it all works out for you. Occasionally D.S.S. does do
right by the system, but after hearing what you all have told
me, I do believe that they have their heads up their
collective asses on this one. Off the record, of course."

They all smiled and nodded knowingly, especially
Ted. He'd seen the Department at work and knew that even
a Judges' teenage daughter wasn't immune to their Gestapo
like tactics. The three of them then thanked Judge Sawyer
and left for their appointment.

Armed with the temporary custody papers and
Ted's experience, they made their way to their next stop.
The Department of Social Services office building. Work
place of Ann Randall and her toady, Patty Strickend. On
the way, Ted reminded them to stay calm and not overreact.
These people love to get parents in your situation angry and
riled up. They believe it helps their case, to show the court
that you can't handle your temper leads them to proving
that you are an abuser. Again he also reminded them to let
him do the talking. Pam and Nick sat in the back seat,
holding hands and listening to Ted. To say they were
worried would be an understatement.

Ted, Judge Sawyer, hell even Ann Randall herself,
all made it clear that D.S.S. calls the shots. Forget that
families are destroyed and lives ruined, as long as it looks
good on paper. Welcome to modern America.

They turned the car onto Westbrook and took an

immediate right into the parking lot of the D.S.S. building.

Nick drew in a deep breath and let out a sigh. "Well, I guess this is it."

"We can't thank you enough for all you are doing for us." Pam said.

"Forget it. I love any chance I can get to go up against these self-righteous pricks." Ted smiled at them from the rearview mirror. He slowed into a space and put the car in park. "Put on your game faces, people, it's show time!"

They all got out and walked to the entrance. What they saw through the double doors shocked them. The lobby was overrun with families with their kids of all ages and ethnic groups. They saw the receptionist sitting at her desk behind a bullet proof glass, speaking to the crowd through a microphone like a bank teller at the drive through. All of the doors leading from the lobby to the offices and meeting rooms beyond were locked, with numbered keypads for some secret code above the doorknob on each.

"It looks to me like they have a history of pissing people off here," whispered Pam.

"No kidding!" Nick whispered back, just as stunned. "I saw less locks last night at the jail than these people have!" He pointed at what appeared to be a bullet hole beside a door to the left. "How much of a hint do these people need before they change the way they do things?"

The group paused for a moment before going up the stairs to the second floor. Not much different than the first floor, they noted. Same bullet proof receptionist, same code locked doors all around.

Ted motioned for them to sit down while he walked over to the receptionist's window. Nick watched them talk through the glass for a moment before sitting in a hardback chair next to his wife.

"I'm feeling pretty good about things, Honey." He put his arm around her, "Everything's going to work out."

Pam laid her head on his shoulder and sighed, "I hope so."

Ted came back and sat down across from them... "They'll be out in a few minutes." He looked his friends over. "Don't worry."

Nora had stayed home in order to be available for when Sally's friend's parents dropped her off that afternoon. Pam had called them before they left that morning. Thank God they hadn't seen the news the night before. Pam had told them that there was a change in plans, and could they drop Sally off over at the Anders' house instead of their own. Sally's friend's mom had no problem with that, and said that Sally had been a pleasure to have over. Of course Ted had to promise his wife that he would call her as soon as they got some answers.

In the second floor lobby of the D.S.S. office, Nick and Pam stiffened as the door in front of them buzzed and then opened. Nick was getting sick of that sound. Out walked Patty Strickend. She looked around the lobby before her eyes found the Roaniks. There was obvious confusion on her face as she searched the room for a nine year old girl.

Nick nudged Ted and pointed towards Patty. Standing up, Ted was a very imposing six foot three. Although it wouldn't take much, Nick thought, to intimidate this drooling little mouse.

"Ms. Strickend?" Ted held out his hand. "My name is Ted Anders. I'll be representing the Roaniks in this matter."

Patty timidly shook his hand and looked past him at Pam hopefully. She didn't want to screw this up and already two things were wrong. First was this giant of a lawyer towering over her, and second, there was no little girl by the name of Sally Nelson in the room. Patty suddenly started to re-think her career choice.

"Um, Mrs. Roanik," she began as unthreatening as possible. She well remembered the tongue lashing she received from the woman the night before. "I thought we were clear last night when we talked about bringing your... um, daughter in here this morning."

Ted was smiling now. As a lawyer he was good at

sizing up his opponents. Right now he sensed fear. Fear from the short, stocky woman in the black pants suit. Fear was good in an opponent in Ted's eyes. It meant weakness. If this woman was the best that they were going to throw at him, then he was actually disappointed. He loved a challenge. Actually thrived on it, that's why he became a lawyer. He loved the game, and he was smart enough to know that this wasn't all that D.S.S. had for him to go up against. No, he knew these people worked together in teams. This was just one social worker in the murky pond that was D.S.S. Beyond the door that she was blocking, would be the team that had been assigned to his friends. The opposing team. He was ready.

"Well, hold on there, little lady," he said in the softest, most patronizing voice he could muster, "Let's not get into this private matter out here in the lobby. Surely you have some more appropriate meeting rooms somewhere. Perhaps even some coffee?" Ted was in the zone.

"Yes Sir. I'm sorry, please, follow me." Patty stammered.

Ted held the door for Nick and Pam. All they could do was shake their heads in disbelief as they passed.

The small but determined group followed Patty through a maze of cubicles that surprisingly were mostly empty. No time to sit around at your desk when there's perfectly good families out there to destroy, thought Pam with disgust. They turned the corner and came to another metal door. Patty opened it and ushered the group into a large room with long, school cafeteria style tables shaped into a square. Conference style. At the end closest to the door, prepared for a quick escape, thought Nick as he passed, sat Ann Randall and two other women. One blond who looked to be in her mid forties, whose wardrobe indicated that she couldn't accept that fact, turned out to be their 'team' leader, Becky Donnaly. Next to her was an older woman, at least fifty-five, with a look of pure mean on her face. At the introductions they found out her name was Justine Woodward and that she was assigned to be their family's social worker.

On the next section of the square was Danny. Sitting next to him was someone from The New Hope Runaway Shelter. A young lady whose name they didn't catch. Linda something or other.

Patty sat down next to Ann and quickly began whispering to her as Ted and his clients sat together on the third side of the square, opposite Danny and his guard. Pam gasped when she saw how swollen and discolored her son's nose had gotten since she last saw him. Nick pulled her closer and kissed her temple. Danny saw all this and cringed in disgust at their display. Whore! he thought to himself. He was spared of anyone seeing the look on his face by Ann Randall as she spoke to the Roaniks.

What Goes Around   by Mick Woodhall

"We've already talked to Danny while we were waiting for you to arrive, and we found out some very disturbing things, Mr. And Mrs. Roanik." Ann shuffled her notes. "We're glad you brought your attorney, we want to do this right. Now please, Mr. Roanik, would you start by telling us about why you've been forcing your stepson to masturbate for you beside the basement furnace?"

CHAPTER III

The room was silent, all but the subtle sound of Danny's sobs as he cried on Linda's bosom. She held him in her arms but her steely gaze, like everyone else in the room, was fixed on Nick.

"What the hell are you talking about?!" Was all Nick could stammer. Ted gave him a look telling him with his eyes to stay in control.

"Are you denying that you know anything about this?" Ann was showing her impatience. A typical D.S.S. tactic used to keep parents on edge.

Pam kept her eyes glued to the table in front of her. She remembered Nick mentioning something about catching Danny masturbating in the basement a year or so ago, but what was this 'forcing' shit they were talking about?

"Ms. Randall?" Danny managed to choke back his tears. "Do I have to sit through this? I fear for my safety just being in the same room as them. Can't Linda take me back to the shelter? This is very painful for me." He pleaded.

"Yes, yes, of course, you've been through so much, you poor thing." Ann consoled him while glaring at the Roaniks' with contempt. "Linda, we'll contact you with our placement decision after we finish up here. Thank you both."

Linda pulled a tissue from her purse and handed it to Danny. He thanked her and wiped his nose with it.

Nick glared at him as he walked out. "And the Academy gives the award for best actor in a dramatic role to Danny Nelson for his portrayal of an abused child in, 'Screw the Parents.'" Nick whispered to Ted.

"You were saying, Mr. Roanik, how often are you in the practice of forcing your stepson to touch himself for you?" Ann asked again.

"Now let's just watch the accusations, Ms. Randall." Ted to the rescue. "Anyone can tell that kid is lying. Anyone with half a brain, that is."

"Children don't normally lie about these things, Mr. Anders, and even if he was lying, we also have the physical abuse. You saw his nose. Something is definitely going on here, and we intend to get to the bottom of it."

"Then let's *do* get to the bottom of it, Ms. Randall, and look at all angles of what's going on. As professionals, we need to take into account every aspect of this matter for the sake of all parties involved. Not just taking the word of a kid who already has a history of delinquent behavior, as well as a police record."

Ann Randall looked as if she had been kicked in the stomach. This was her turf. Who did this guy think he was to come in to her office and question her professionalism? In front of her subordinates no less. It was safe to say that Ann did not like Ted Anders. Oh, she respected him, but she did not like him.

"It's all right, Ted," Nick broke the stand- off, "Ms. Randall, I am not now, nor have I ever been, in the practice of forcing anyone to masturbate for my viewing pleasure. I not only find what you are insinuating to be insulting, it is disgusting as well. I will tell you that there was this one time, when I had gone down into our basement for a tool or something, I can't remember what. I heard a noise over by the furnace," Nick looked thoughtful, "a moaning sound. So I went over to see what it was, and there was Danny. Already into the act. I assure you, I was just as embarrassed as the boy. Probably more so."

"You see Ms. Randall," Ted began, "teenage boys play with themselves. It's perfectly normal. Danny just happened to get caught and fabricated this whole story to avoid embarrassment. I have to admit, I don't understand the whole furnace thing, but to each their own. Now, can we stop this whole witch hunt you've got us on and deal with the issues at hand?"

"Well forced or not, the truth is," sniffed Ann, "we have two different stories here, and a kid with one hell of a swollen nose." She paused and looked at her colleagues. "The team that has been assigned to your case has decided that until these matters are settled, Danny is to stay with his biological father," she thumbed through her notes, "a Mr. Jeff Nelson." She looked up at them.

Pam gasped. "Do you have any idea what you're doing to that child?!"

"Hold on, Pam!" Ted whispered to his client.

"We feel it is in Danny's best interest, and for his safety, to remove him from his step-father's influence, Mrs. Roanik, and from what we've seen, you refuse to even consider Danny's side in all of this. You choose to blame him, us, everyone but yourselves. I'm sorry, but we have to consider the child's well being first."

"By sending him to live with a necrophiliac?" Pam stood up. Ted's fear had happened. These people definitely knew how to push the right buttons. Pam continued, "How is that going to help him?" She almost screamed it.

Ann smiled, "Be careful, Mrs. Roanik, an alleged necrophiliac. According to our records the charge was never substantiated so we can't use it as a basis to deny placement." Ann was truly loving this. "Mr. Nelson is

Danny's natural father, so unless you have a legitimate objection as to why he can't stay there, we need to move on. Now, about Sally. Where is she?" They all turned to Ted.

Ted explained what they had done regarding Sally, and before Ann and her lynch mob could object, he gave her a copy of the Judge's order. Ted got quite a bit of satisfaction from the shade of red Ann's face turned as anger overcame her.

"Of course you know, we'll be having our attorneys look into the legality of this move, Mr. Anders. Mrs. Roanik, Justine will be by to see you twice a month. Unannounced." Ann bitterly continued, "We will also be petitioning the Judge for a court order regarding certain programs we'll require the two of you to attend, starting with a D.S.S. approved program for anger management, as well as parenting classes." She then stood up, and showing no sign of defeat, collected the paper work. "We'll be in touch, good-bye."

As Ann left the room, Nick and Pam stared at the rest of the D.S.S. dream team, while they got up, and one by one, quietly followed her out. The last thing they heard was Ann telling the team leader to get in contact with Jeff Nelson and make arrangements for Danny.

Nick and Pam both let out a sigh of relief. Sally was safe. At least for now. What about Danny? Couldn't they see the mistake they were making? Didn't they see his fingers tapping on the table like crazy the whole time he did his 'woe is me' act? He needed help. Not the kind a drunk, corpse fucker could give. Even if the drunk corpse fucker was the boy's father. Pam was visibly shook up. She didn't care if it was never proven. She knew Jeff. She knew he did it. Probably more than once.

Jeff Nelson took a taxi from his trailer to the New Hope Runaway Shelter to pick up his son. He had lost his license a couple of years back, due to several D.U.Is.

"This is becoming a pattern, Mr. Nelson. A pattern that I'm going to put a stop to before you kill yourself or someone else," Judge Sawyer had told him after the last one, just before he revoked his license. It didn't bother Jeff though. Right now he was just happy to be getting his son back. That meant he was one step closer to getting his wife back. Jeff knew that the kids were Pam's life. She couldn't bear to be without her precious babies. Now she would stop being a whore with that bastard Nick, and come home where she belonged. Yeah, buddy!

Jeff couldn't believe his ears when Becky something or other called and told him that Danny would be coming to live with him. Why, he almost dropped his beer when she said it. Almost. Of course he knew it would happen. It was just a matter of time before that prick screwed up. Who did he think he was anyway? Nick the newscaster? Nick the child abusing wife-stealer was more like it. Jeff wished he still had his practice. He'd kill that fuck stick Nick and then fuck him up his embalmed ass. Jeff had never fucked a dead man before. After all, he wasn't gay, but that was just what Nick deserved for stealing his whore wife. That's what whore stealers get. Yeah, buddy, fucked up their dead embalmed ass, Jeff thought. A wad of my sperm, swimming through his decayed body all the way to hell!

"Is everything all right, Sir?" The cab driver looked at Jeff through the rearview mirror.

"What? Oh, yeah!" Jeff smiled and settled back into the seat. "Everything's going to be just great!"

The cab pulled into the parking lot next to the two story brick building where Danny was staying. Jeff told the driver to wait on him and climbed out of the back seat. He walked the short distance to the front door and rang the bell.

Looking at his reflection in the glass, Jeff thought he resembled a Viking. With his unruly mass of red hair and the shaggy red beard he had grown after the divorce, he could favor an old Norseman. However, when you add the protruding beer belly that he had also been working on since the divorce, you came to realize that the only Viking he really favored was Hagar the Horrible from the comic

68

strip.

After the second knock on the door Linda answered. "Can I help you, sir?" she asked, slightly wary of the man standing in front of her.

"Um, yeah. I'm here to pick up my son. Danny Nelson. I'm Jeff Nelson." Although gruff in appearance these days, when he was sober, Jeff could still muster up that soothing funeral director's tone.

Linda looked him over. He was not what she had expected as Danny's dad. "Please come in."

Jeff couldn't help but notice the way her firm, round ass bounced under her purple shorts as he followed her into the office. The bounce of a whore, he thought. I bet ol' Dannys' had some of that while he's been here. She can't be more than nineteen years old, tops.

Linda felt his stare and pointed to the couch across from the counselor's desk. "Have a seat." She coldly told him. "I'll let Danny know you're here."

"Thank you, miss." Jeff said, knowing he had been caught, but not caring much. After all, she was the one that was bouncing her ass that way for my enjoyment, right? He justified to himself.

Jeff sat and watched the fish in the aquarium for the few minutes it took Linda to come back with his son.

When Danny came down he couldn't have been happier. His plan was coming together almost perfectly.

Step one had been a success. When the social worker told him about the plan for Sally, he was visibly agitated. That fucking do good lawyer! That was one move Danny hadn't anticipated. It didn't change things though. It might have delayed them a little, but he would deal with that arrogant asshole Anders in due time. Right now he allowed himself to be happy. He understood his dad and his dad understood him. No more dealing with the whore or her phony husband. Well, not today anyway.

That night father and son sat outside Jeff's trailer and celebrated the fact that they were back together. Jeff even cooked on the grill. The best way to eat Spam, he told Danny, is to grill it and put it on toast. Jeff even gave Danny some beer to wash it down with. Just two guys eating Spam sandwiches and drinking cold Budweiser. Life was good, thought Danny.

The two of them talked for hours. Well into the night, as well as deep into the case of beer. Danny told him how stupid Nick looked at the D.S.S. meeting, and how he had to think of his parents divorce to work up the tears he needed to be convincing.

Then he must have had a little too much beer. He'd never drank before, but he didn't want to disappoint his dad when he offered. Danny started to feel light headed. He couldn't stop talking, his inhibitions had left him, and he started telling his dad about Jane. How he still loved her.

Then, when Danny stood up to take a leak, it happened.
The deck started swimming and Danny reached for the rail
to steady it. Too late. In one great rumble from deep within
his stomach, Danny barely opened his mouth before a wet,
foamy, mass of Spam, toast, and mustard, swirling through
the urine color of regurgitated beer, came projecting from
him towards his father. Jeff sat in drunken disbelief as
chunks of his son's dinner clung to his now wet jeans.

He got out of his lawn chair and helped his son over
to the edge of the deck laying him down on his stomach.
His head hung over the side, bobbing above the walkway
leading to his dad's shed. Jeff just managed to position
Danny before the next round came up. "What a waste of
good Spam." Jeff mumbled while going inside for another
beer and to take a leak. By the time he came back outside,
Danny had puked two more times and had managed to roll
over so he was on his back with his head leaning against
the rail.

Jeff threw him a towel and sat down with his beer.
"You got soft living over there with TV boy. Don't worry,
when we get your mother back, we'll toughen you up
again. Things will be like before, you'll see." He took
another drink and stared off at the stars.

Get your mother back? Danny struggled to clear his
head. What did he mean? I just got rid of that bitch so we
could be together. What about all of the stuff she did to

71

him? All the stuff he had said. About this time Danny passed out. The last thing he heard was his dad slurring over and over, "Oh, yes, she'll pay. When she comes back, she owes me. Big time."

Danny woke up shaking with cold a couple of hours before dawn the next morning. It took him a few minutes to get his bearings, and the sledgehammer in his skull didn't help. He looked to the left and saw the rusty charcoal grill that had last night cooked their feast. "Shit, it's cold!" he said as he pulled his stiff body up from the deck. That was a mistake, as soon as he said it, a light breeze blew his breath back at him, and as he smelled the acrid, hours old vomit, he started heaving again. Steadying himself against the trailer, Danny struggled with dry heaves for a couple of minutes. Suddenly, he was grateful for the cool breeze. The aroma of the dried up bile in front of his dad's chair from the night before made his head spin.

What the hell does Dad find so enjoyable about drinking anyway? Danny thought after he caught his breath. Then, looking around, he wondered where his dad was. Danny opened the front door and stepped into the warmth of the trailer. Sure enough, there was Jeff, asleep in his chair with a spilled can of beer at his feet.

Why didn't he bring me inside? It may be June, but everyone knows how chilly the mountain air is early in the morning. Danny was hurt. It's not like he didn't want the mess of me throwing up in his house. Looking at his Dad with disgust, he noticed Jeff was still wearing the same jeans that Danny had puked on earlier. Only now, the Spam chunks had dried and shriveled up. They looked like pink raisins dangling from his Dad's stained pants. Danny looked again at the worn spot in front of his Dad's chair from where years of spilled beer had eaten away the carpet. No, pride of his home and cleanliness were definitely not Jeff's reason for leaving his sick son outside all night in the cold.

Danny looked away and went to his backpack, which was still full and laying in the corner of the living room where he threw it when they arrived. Un-zipping the outer pocket, he pulled out his toothbrush and paste and went into the bathroom. He couldn't stand the taste in his mouth any longer, let alone his breath. As he brushed, his thoughts wandered back to Jane. He'd been thinking about her a lot lately. She was the last person he had dated. He never had any desire to see anyone else. No, she was the one. Danny knew it and was getting tired of waiting for her to realize her true feelings and come crawling back to him.

Danny spit the foamy toothpaste into the sink and rinsed his mouth. He remembered that Jane had gone out with another guy after Eddie Jenkins went to jail. This was painful to Danny and it made him angry. Why hadn't she learned her lesson? he questioned.

73

  The guy she dated then was Randy Dawson. Danny knew him some. They used to hang out sometimes and play ball. That was before Randy told Danny that he wanted to ask Jane out. Randy knew that the two of them used to go out, so he wanted to know if Danny was cool with it. Through a mask of contempt, Danny told him to do whatever he wanted. He had to say it twice though, because Randy couldn't hear him over all the finger tapping that Danny was doing as he mumbled it. Randy ignored the tapping once he understood what his friend had said. He was too jazzed to worry about obsessive behavior.

  Maybe worry was what he should have done. It wasn't long after that when D.S.S. took Randy away from his mother. Danny called their house the day they took Randy to foster care and found him hysterical. Apparently, D.S.S. was convinced that Randy's mother was molesting him, and had been for some time. His mom denied it of course, and Randy couldn't convince the idiots that no, she never touched his penis, and no, he did not call them anonymously claiming that she did. Danny could hear Randy's mother crying in the background. Poor thing, Danny thought. He had always liked her. Never would have figured her for a pervert.

  Randy was to be sent to a home near Charlotte to live while he and his mother went to required counseling. He wrote Danny and told him that D.S.S. had told him that it would probably take close to two years before his mother could have him back, but the process would go quicker if Randy would quit protecting his mother, and just admit that she molested him so he could begin his healing process. That was the last time Danny heard from him. There's some sick people in this world, Danny thought as he crumbled up the letter and tossed it in the trash.

Finishing up in the bathroom, Danny wiped his mouth and looked at his bloodshot eyes in the mirror. Maybe it was time he helped Jane realize that she still loved him, he thought as his fingers tapped away on the edge of the sink.

"Nick, sit down and quit worrying." The station manager at channel 11 was sitting on the edge of his desk, facing Nick. "We believe you're innocent, and everyone here is pulling for you. However, you of all people know that the general public doesn't buy into all that innocent until proven guilty bullshit. You know the media helps the people decide a person's fate long before they even enter a courtroom. I don't know how channel 9 got a hold of this, but the minute people saw you leave the jail on TV, you lost respectability. I'm sorry, my hands are tied."

"Look, Ernie," Nick pleaded, "I've been giving the people in this area the news for years. The viewers believe in me."

"Nick," his boss sighed, "the station can't take that risk, we're already losing advertisers. Hell, we've even had a call from that Celebrity Boxing show." He paused a moment and stood up. "Nick, we go back a long way, so I hope you don't take offense to what I'm about to say. We covered for you when Danny vandalized the building. Your last names were different so no connections were made. This time it's different. It's blown wide open. Hell, child abuse?" Nick's boss shook his head and let out a sigh. "We both know that most teenagers need a good kick in the ass now and then, but this is a different country than when we were young. Hell, my dad used a switch to keep me in line."

"Damn it, Ernie!" Nick interrupted, "You're talking like you actually think I did it. I never touched him. By the time I got home it was over!"

"Yeah, you told me. Danny hit himself. Did you see it, or is that what Pam told you?"

"Why do people keep asking me that? Pam told me! So what. The point is that I never touched him. God knows I want to now, though." Nick's hands were clenched on the arms of his chair.

"I'm sorry Nick, like I said, my hands are tied. As of today you're on suspension until this matter is settled." Ernie Hudson walked back around his desk and sat down. "Look at it positively, Nick. Take Pam on a vacation. Relax

76

a little. You'll be fine. Come and see me if anything
changes."

Nick knew there wasn't anymore to say. Why is all
this happening to me, he thought as he walked out of the
station, towards his car. He needed to think, sort some
things out in his head. His car found its way out of the
parking lot and in the direction of the Foghorn bar across
town.

The Foghorn was this little dive of a bar that made
the best burgers and everybody left you alone. Tom Cruise
could walk in and no one would bat an eye. Nick went
there whenever he wanted to be alone, or to think
something through. Most of the people that hung out at the
Foghorn had their own problems to deal with. Mostly poor
or out of work, Nick doubted that many of them knew who
he was. Very few of them looked like they owned
televisions, and the few that did appeared the type to prefer
wrestling or Baywatch reruns over the evening news. That
was just fine with Nick.

He parked in the gravel lot and went through the
double glass doors that were tinted blue with a foghorn
painted on one and a lighthouse on the other. Waiting by
the cigarette machine in the entrance way for his eyes to
adjust to the dim yellowish bar lighting, he thought about
what his boss had asked him. 'Is that what you saw, or did
Pam tell you that?" Ernie had asked. Someone else had

asked him that, but whom?

When he could see clearly again, Nick made his way past the juke box and heard Jimmy Buffet singing about changes in latitudes. Not Buffet's finest in Nick's opinion, but catchy none the less. He nodded absently at two elderly men arguing over a pool game. Something about not calling a shot properly was all Nick heard as he walked by, making his way to the bar.

Settling onto the torn, blue plastic covered stool, he stared listlessly at the rows of bottles lined up along the back of the bar. Step right up folks! All your cares and concerns will quickly disappear with our magic potions! Name your color. Name your flavor! The carnival barker hawking his cocktails in Nick's mind was quickly interrupted by Sheila, the Foghorns answer to Cheers' Sam Malone. Her husky voice, deep and craggy from years of Newports and scotch, could be heard from clear over at the other end of the bar.

"Hey, Nick!" She walked past a man and woman huddled together about six stools down and was now facing Nick dead on. "Kinda early today, huh? What can I get ya?" she coughed.

Nick looked at his watch. It *was* kind of early. Hell, it's not like I have to be at work or anything, he thought bitterly. "Let me get one of your famous bacon cheeseburgers with fries and a bottle of Michelob Light,

Sheila." He mustered up a smile as he ordered. "Oh yeah, and a shot of Cuervo."

"Having a rough day, Hon?" She smiled and patted his hand. She looked a lot younger than her fifty-four years when she smiled, but Nick had always seen a lot of years of hurt in her brown eyes.

"I've been better." He tilted the shot glass she had placed in front of him.

"I saw you on the news the other night," she leaned towards him. "For what it's worth, I don't believe a bit of that shit they're accusing you of. In all the years you've been coming in here, you've always been a perfect gentleman. Shame on all those people sayin' all that nonsense about a guy like you."

"Thank you, Sheila. It does mean a lot to me, but I could still use another shot."

She patted his arm again and poured the tequila before going back to the kitchen to give his order to the cook. Some greasy haired high school drop-out with an endless supply of torn Eminem tee shirts no doubt, Nick thought. Sheila was the one constant figure there at the Foghorn. The cooks changed almost as often as the fryer grease.

After Nick's second round of tequila, he started to feel a little better. Singing quietly along with The Doors' *Break on Through* coming from the juke box he began to

79

relax. After a few minutes and well into Bob Seger's *Turn The Page* (a far superior version than the Metallica re-make that the interns were always playing on their lunch breaks at the station) the cook set a burger on the bar in front of Nick. The newscaster picked up a french fry and watched the cook go back into the kitchen. Nick had been close. Only the tee-shirt was Led Zeppelin, instead of Eminem. Old school drop-out, he told himself as he chewed on the fry.

By the time Nick had finished his burger he had downed two more beers and was waiting on Sheila to bring him his after burger shot to round out his afternoon. Looking around, he noticed a few more people had come in. Mostly old retired men, drinking away their savings so their ungrateful children wouldn't inherit it when they finally die. Probably from liver failure. Frank Sinatra was doing it his way in the background now and Nick was starting to feel numb.

"Pick your color, pick your flavor. All the booze for you to savor." The carnival barker was working the mid-way again. In this case, the mid-way being the worn out Foghorn bar for worn out men. Ladies welcome, of course. "Tequila, rum and sweet vermouth, help forget what ails you!" Nick's head was swimming.

"Nick? I thought that was you!" A man in a blue sport coat, over a tee-shirt and jeans approached him.

Great, thought Nick as the barker faded back into his mind. "On top of everything else, I'm being harassed by Huey Lewis," he mumbled.

"Very funny, Pal!" The man took the stool next to him and briefly frowned at the stack of empty shot glasses piling up in front of Nick.

Following his gaze, Nick grumbled, "Dishwasher must be on break. Can I help you?"

If Charlie Tibbens was shocked that Nick didn't remember him, he didn't show it. After all, in his line of work the poker face was essential. "Charlie Tibbens. You know, from jail."

Nick looked around and noticed a few other customers had heard this, and were now looking at the two of them curiously. "Mind keeping your voice down, Charlie?" Nick asked sarcastically while taking another drink from his bottle.

"Yeah, sure, anyway, how ya been?"

"Let's see, in the past week I've been arrested, humiliated, lost two kids and my job. How the hell do you think I've been?" Nick dismissed him with the shot of tequila Sheila set in front of him.

"I don't think that's going to help." Charlie replied, now looking at yet another empty shot glass.

"Look, I don't know how you found me here, and I don't mean to be rude, but I've got enough friends already.

Most of whom have never seen the inside of a jail cell, let alone consider it a part of their job description. So, please excuse me, I've got some things on my mind." Nick stared at him.

None of this fazed Charlie. He was used to being told in many different ways to 'fuck off'. Usually he didn't. "First of all, tough guy, I didn't follow you here. I was checking out a lead on a case I'm working on and was nearby. I got hungry and stopped in for some lunch. Secondly, while spending time in jail is *not* in my job description, dealing with assholes who think that just because they have money or fame that they're better than us lowly peasants, unfortunately is."

Nick felt the sting. He never thought of himself as stuck-up or better than others. Hell, just because I'm having a string of bad luck, he thought, it's not his fault.

"Point taken. I apologize. Let me buy you a drink, Charlie." Nick said.

"That's better, Jack and Coke, my dear lady." All smiles again, Charlie ordered from Sheila.

"You got it, you smooth talker." She teased back from down the bar.

"So, did you get that child support ordeal straightened out?" Nick asked as casual as he could.

"I thought you said you lost your job, why the interrogation then?" Charlie winked.

Not casual enough I guess, thought Nick. "Well you know, once a reporter…"

Charlie chuckled at him. "Yeah, everything's OK with that now. How about you? Stepson still kicking his own ass?"

Nick shot him a look. "He's gone to live with his father for awhile."

"D.S.S. or y'all?" Charlie asked.

"D.S.S. made the call, but you know," Nick said thoughtfully, "I suspect it was what he wanted all along. He and I never connected. He's close to his mother though."

"How'd she take the decision?" Charlie had finished his drink and was trying to signal Sheila for a refill.

"Not well. The guy's a bum. I did a story on him several years ago. Had it all. Great wife, fantastic kids, a promising career. Owned his own funeral home. Then he supposedly got caught screwing a corpse and he lost everything. His business, home, Pam and the kids. Last I heard he sits in his ratty old trailer drinking beer all day. So, no, Pam doesn't like Danny being there at all."

When Sheila came over for Charlie, Nick ordered another beer. He figured he'd had enough tequila for one afternoon.

"Man, that's rough. I think I remember that guy. Never could prove it, right? His life was ruined none the less. No wonder he turned to the bottle."

Nick gave him another look as Sheila sat their drinks in front of them.

"Seems like a lot of things happen concerning Danny and his mom that can't be proven." Charlie muttered thoughtfully as he sipped his drink.

"What the hell does that mean?" Nick was losing his composure. Who was this guy? Comes in to my life dressed like an 80's pop star and starts making accusations about my family, Nick fumed.

"Now don't take offense, Nick. I was just comparing the two scenarios, that's all. Hell, I don't know any more about your family than what you've told me, but think about it. When I sat down here today, what did you say to me?"

"Um, leave me the hell alone. Was that it?" Nick snapped and turned back to his beer.

Charlie shook his head. "Besides that. No, you said you've been arrested, humiliated, lost your kids and your job. Sounds like a pattern, huh? Sorry, like you said, once an investigator…"

"The two aren't the same. My wife was there when Danny went nuts and hit himself…" Nick was overwhelmed.

"I know. She told you. Was she there when her ex, what's his name, used someone's dead aunt as his personal blow-up doll? I mean did anyone witness it?"

Nick couldn't answer. All this was too much to think about, and the tequila wasn't helping. His mind was fogging over. Charlie was wrong. Pam wasn't responsible for the mess they were in. It wouldn't make sense. She lost her son, and her daughter has to stay with the Anders' for God knows how long. The loss of Nick's job would affect her as well. No way. Maybe this bullshit was Charlie Tibbens' way of drumming up business.

"Look Charlie," Nick said while pulling out his wallet, "you've definitely given me some things to think about…"

Charlie recognized the patronizing tone at once. "I'm sorry Nick. I guess I really should learn to keep my mouth shut. I tend to live my job and it has a way of fucking up friendships. Forget I said anything. I tend to find a conspiracy in just about everything. No hard feelings?" Charlie offered his hand.

Nick swallowed the last gulp of beer and shook Charlie's hand as he stood up.

"Not everyone has a dark side Obi-wan," Said Nick. "Some couples are genuinely in love and just happen to run into some unfortunate circumstances. Maybe I'll see you again." Nick walked out without waiting for a response.

Charlie looked after him for a minute before signaling Sheila for another drink. They all start out in denial, he thought. Who wants to think that the love of their life isn't quite the person they've pretended to be for so many years? Charlie took a large gulp of the whiskey. Oh, and yes, Nicky Skywalker, everyone does have a dark side. Some are just better at controlling it. Then Charlie raised his glass in the air and whispered, "May the force be with you, Buddy. You're gonna need it."

Pam Roanik was more relaxed at the moment than her husband. She lay naked in a bed about fifteen miles from the bar that Nick had just left. The bed lay in room 216 of the Mount Vernon Motel and Breakfast Nook, just off of Interstate 40.

She stretched her body and felt the tingling sensation on her nipples as the sheet slid across her supple breasts. The sex had been good, she smiled. Like it used to be with Nick in the beginning, when he took the time to please her. Pam sat up and pulled her knees to her chest with the sheet over them and reached for her glass of champagne from the night stand.

Damn that Nick. She thought as she took a sip. Always focused on his career, just like Jeff was. He knew what had happened to her. They both did. They knew she needed more attention. Needed to feel that she was number one in someone's life. Bastards! Just like all men. They promise the world then cum in your mouth. Isn't that what her daddy had told her for all those years? He was even nice enough to show her, and he showed her often because little girls don't always remember the lessons that their parents teach them the first time. Pam did remember. She remembered how that awful stuff tasted. How her father would pinch her nose and hold her mouth until she had to swallow it or suffocate.

"Yes daddy, I remember all you taught me," she muttered.

Pam came back to the present with the sound of the shower turning off and a man's whistling in the bathroom. Clicking off the television with the remote that was bolted to a swivel bar on the night stand, she wondered why the men in her life always showered right after they made love to her. Maybe she really was as dirty as her father had always said. Or maybe all men are egocentric bastards who use innocent little girls and women as their personal cum dumpsters. She took a bigger swig from her glass and glared at the bathroom door. By the time it opened Pam had calmed down and was her old self again.

"You were incredible, baby," said the man as he sat on the bed beside her.

"You were pretty good yourself." Pam smiled as Ted Anders pulled her into his arms and kissed her.

CHAPTER IV

Pam looked into Ted's eyes and told him she couldn't thank him enough for letting Sally stay with them.

He kissed her nose and slid under the sheets next to her. "Happy to do it, sweetie. She's a great kid. Nora adores her. Besides, it gives me a chance to see more of you."

"You sound just like my father."

"Well," Ted responded, "I hope that's a good thing."

Pam didn't answer. Typical bastard, she thought, use an innocent child as an excuse to get his dick wet. "I've got to go. Nick will be home soon." She climbed out of the bed and wrapped the sheet around her naked body as she walked to the bathroom, giving Ted one last peek at her firm ass.

Ted called to her from the bed and when she turned around, he opened the towel he had wrapped around him so she could see him rising to his full length again. "Are you sure that you don't have time for another go, sweetie? You sure look hot in that sheet."

"I'd love to, honey," Pam gave him a cynical smile, "but you know the area is in a drought and it would be irresponsible on my part to cause you to have to take another shower." Pam turned back around and went into the bathroom, closing the door behind her. She wondered how good of a lawyer Ted could be when he couldn't recognize sarcasm when it was right in his face.

Pam got dressed and freshened up some, but didn't bother to shower. She looked how Ted had left it, hair all over the soap, towels everywhere. She was too disgusted to use it. Besides, they had used a condom and it had been a very long time since Nick had jumped her bones when he first got home. She looked again at the dirty tub. At home, where it's clean is where I'll shower. Pam told herself.

When she came out of the bathroom, Ted was already dressed. Blue suit, power tie, ready for business. They kissed before looking out the door and around the parking lot.

"Coast is clear, let's go." Pam left first, leaving Ted to wait fifteen more minutes until she was well on her way before he started for his car.

She's a damn good fuck, he thought. She runs a little hot and cold though. Oh well, that's a woman for you. Ted reached his car and scanned the area one last time before getting in. This was a seedy part of town. The other side of the tracks, as they say. He was slightly concerned about being seen by one of the degenerates he sometimes represents.

He pulled out of the lot and took the side street to the access ramp onto I-40. He had to get back to his office to work on Nick's case. After all, it was the least he could do after screwing the hell out of his friend's wife.

Jeff Nelson was hot. Hot and sweaty. He was glad that this would be the last day of his latest batch of community service. He was sick to death of picking up roadside trash.

He had left Danny back at the trailer to sleep off his hangover. I should have brought him with me today, Jeff thought; make a man out of him. Puking up perfectly good Spam after only a few beers. Damn that boy. Stained my favorite Marlboro tee-shirt with all that Linda Blair projectile shit. The hotter the day got, the madder Jeff got.

"That kid needs to get a job! Hell, it's summer and he's damn sure old enough! Yeah, buddy…" Jeff began.

"Quit yer damn bitchin', Cracker, before I make you mine!"

Jeff looked over at the big black guy in the orange vest next to him. He didn't realize he'd been saying all that shit out loud. "Come on James," smiled Jeff, "you know

I'll just break your heart."

"You crazy white boy." James Pearson slapped Jeff's back. Harder than Jeff cared for, but he kept quiet. James straightened up and looked down the access road that the eight man crew was working on. "A lot of damn used rubbers layin' around here. Fucking motel right across the street. Cheap sons of bitches." He wiped the bead of sweat off of his nose that was threatening to fall at any second.

Jeff stretched and cracked his neck. "Probably teenagers, can't afford a room."

They both stood there for a second squinting in the sun, looking across the street at the Mount Vernon Motel and Breakfast Nook. It was well past breakfast and the restaurant was closed. Just seeing it made Jeff's stomach growl.

"I'm fucking starving. When do we break for lunch?" Jeff moaned.

"Holy shit, I'd like to eat that." James whistled, pointing at an attractive woman crossing the motel parking lot towards her car.

When Jeff's gaze followed James' finger, all thoughts of hunger left him. Well, what the fuck is this! He thought as he covered his eyes from the sun. It can't be! Yeah, buddy! It is! What the hell is Pam doing at a motel way the fuck out here? Jeff watched her get into her car and drive away. He turned to pick up a wadded burger wrapper so she wouldn't recognize him as she passed onto the freeway.

"Damn, that was some sweet white meat!" declared James, who hadn't bothered to be discreet. He watched her the whole time.

Jeff scanned the parking lot. Four other cars still there and one had to be the desk clerk's, Jeff decided. With another probably belonging to the housekeeper. Small motel, probably only one. The restaurant had been closed for a couple of hours, so all the people working there would be long gone. That left two cars. People don't go to out of the way motels in the middle of the day alone. Pam had left alone, so that meant someone met the whore there. But who? Jeff scanned the cars again. A beat-up pick-up truck, a newer model blue Mustang, a white Lincoln Town car, and someone's rusted attempt to relive Smokey and the Bandit's glory days with an old Trans-am. Jeff knew Pam's obsession with cleanliness and order and eliminated the rust bucket and pick-up. That left the Mustang and Lincoln.

"Get busy, Nelson!" The officer in charge had noticed Jeff's lack of enthusiasm for the job at hand.

Jeff bent over and picked up a used tampon. Probably came out of your ass, was his thought as he tossed it into the bag. Out of the corner of his eye he kept watch on the motel.

After a few minutes a nice looking man who looked to be in his mid-thirties came out of a room on the second floor. He was nicely dressed and walked with a certain confidence.

This could be the one, Jeff thought. Definitely looks like that whores type. His interest rose even more when the man opened the Mustang. Something caught the sun in the corner of Jeff's vision as he watched the man take the top down on his car. He looked towards the reflection and saw a woman in a tennis dress coming out of the room the man just left. Jeff watched her blow a kiss to Mustang Man and thought, damn, is that all these people have to do in the afternoon? Don't they have jobs? That was definitely not who Pam was with. She'd do a lot of things in bed but she never went in for the whole group thing before. Jeff doubted she'd changed that much since their divorce.

"Let's see who our next contestant will be!" he mumbled while picking up another fast food wrapper.

Roughly fifteen minutes later Jeff spotted another well dressed man coming out of a room. Jeff knew he had his man. The way he casually scanned the parking lot and road before he fully emerged made him look guilty as hell. He's hiding from something or someone, Jeff told himself. The man then, apparently satisfied with his visual search, closed the room door and walked towards the stairs leading down to the parking lot. He's probably hiding from his wife, Jeff smiled. Prove me right Lover-boy, which one is it? Jeff stopped working again and focused his attention on which car the businessman would approach.

Jeff's grinned broadened to reveal his cigarette stained teeth when his hunch proved right and the man in the blue suit put his key in the lock of the Lincoln.

"Damn whore, I knew it!" Jeff was jumping up and down, waving his arms in the air. He looked like a deranged kangaroo.

"Nelson!" The officer was beside him again. "Just what in the hell do you think you are doing? Unless your balls are on fire you sure as shit better stop that jumping around and get back to work!"

"Yes, Sir!" exclaimed Jeff, stopping the jumping but he kept grinning. "Can I borrow your pen for just one second, please? I just remembered something and I need to write it down."

The officer glared at him for a few seconds then pulled the pen from his shirt pocket, "Make it quick Ass-wipe, and then get back to work."

Jeff took the pen and fished around in his orange trash bag until he pulled out an old stained match-book. Looking past the officer's shoulder, he caught the tag number of the Lincoln as it drove past. As discretely as possible, he wrote down the number in the match-book and gave the guard back his pen. Jeff didn't know what he was

94

going to do with the information yet, but he did know it was valuable. He put the match-book in his pocket and went back to work on what was turning out to be a damn fine day. A damn fine day indeed.

Danny was glad that his dad had some stuff to do. He still felt lousy and wanted to recover in peace. He hadn't thrown up again, but his stomach was still touchy and his head throbbed. Yep, it was better if he just kicked around the house for awhile. He wished his dad had cable. All the rabbit ears picked up were PBS and Nick's station.

Danny needed to figure out a way to get some personal things from his mom's house. He didn't think he'd have too much trouble conning the social worker into taking him back over there to pick them up. Just as long as the old bitch was with him to protect him from those evil people. Danny laughed quietly.

Those people at D.S.S. are more gullible than Danny had ever imagined. Sure, he had some friends that called social services on their own parents when they couldn't go to a party or some such lame bullshit, but to believe that a well respected news anchor actually forces his stepson to masturbate for him? That was a stretch even Danny couldn't believe they bought. Dumbasses!

Oh well, the fucker deserved it, thought Danny while pouring some soda into a glass. That'll teach him to sneak up on people. What was he doing in the basement that day, anyway? He never goes down there. Hell, maybe he *is* a pervert. Pervert marries whore. News at eleven. That thought made Danny laugh so hard that the soda came out of his nose.

After a while Danny started feeling better. Looking in the cupboard for something to eat only brought disappointment, and a slight return of the nausea. Cans of Spam, potted meat, and Vienna sausages were about his only choices. He opted for a piece of dry bread instead.

Early in the afternoon he finally ventured outside. Sunglasses were a must. As he walked across the deck, he was careful to avoid looking at or stepping in the pile of vomit that was baking in the June sun. Maybe it will rain, he thought. That'll wash that shit outta my sight.

He walked around the trailer park to see what was going on. Three trailers down from his dad's was a young woman hanging clothes on a line as two toddlers ran around her. Danny couldn't help but stop and admire her in her tight cut-offs. He noticed that all of the clothes that she was hanging were either women's or children's. He watched the two kids almost trip the woman as they circled her.

Danny didn't much care for little kids. His sister was all right, as far as kids went, but that was about it.

Danny watched the woman as she bent into the

clothes basket with her ass peeking out of the bottom of her shorts, and he even enjoyed it as she put her hands over her head to reach the clothes line. He especially liked the way her halter top fell away and he could see the curves of her full breasts. After about the third round of basket to line, Danny started to really get aroused. Unconsciously, his hand went into the pocket of his jeans. He could feel himself getting hard through the thin material of the pocket lining. His mind wandered as he pictured Jane, dressed like the woman doing laundry. He imagined how when she bent over the basket he would come up behind her. His hand started caressing his manhood through his pocket.

"Are you OK?"

Danny opened his eyes and saw that the woman was no longer hanging clothes, but was now standing in front of him with a confused look on her face. She was holding her two children to her side, not yet sure of the teenager on her sidewalk, smiling with his hands in his pockets. With the sunglasses on she probably thought he was some kind of Stevie Wonder wannabe.

Danny's face turned red and his erection disappeared as quickly as it had arrived. "Um, oh, uh, yes ma'am. I was just enjoying the view, I mean the day." He stammered while looking at his tennis shoe.

The woman smiled, obviously flattered. "Yes, the 'view' is nice from here too." She winked.

He allowed himself to look up and meet her eyes. She was even prettier up close, Danny thought. With her blond hair pulled back into a ponytail, she looked even younger than he originally thought. Nineteen, twenty tops.

"Uh, I um, better be going." He shuffled his foot.

"Hey, aren't you Jeff's son? Jeff Nelson, he lives up the road in…"

Danny interrupted her as she pointed to his dad's run down trailer. "Yeah, my name's Danny." He ran his hand across the back of his neck. It was getting hot.

"Do you live with him now? Or just visiting?" she asked while sizing him up. She had eased her grip on the kids and by now they had wiggled away to begin a game of tag back by the clothes line. "By the way, I'm Beth." She thrust her hand out to him. As Danny shook it he explained that, yes he was staying with his dad, but he wasn't sure for how long.

"Hard to believe you're his son," she commented, "you don't look at all like him."

Danny didn't know if she meant that as a compliment or not, but judging from her smile, he thought so.

"Look, Danny was it? I'm about done here and it's getting pretty hot out, how about some lemonade?"

Before he could object, she added, "I don't get a lot of company. I moved here not that long ago myself and you're one of the few people I've met in the neighborhood." She reached up and pulled her ponytail away from her neck and sighed when the slight breeze touched the hot spot where it had been hanging. "I could really use some adult conversation, if you know what I mean." She pointed at the two toddlers, one of whom was being tied to a tree by the other.

Danny looked at the clothes line again. It was pretty clear that whatever man had been involved in this scenario was gone now. No worries there. Besides, she made him feel good; calling him an 'adult' even though he was only seventeen.

"Okay Beth, I guess it would be all right. I am kind of thirsty." He knew what was in his dad's fridge, and lemonade sounded a hell of a lot better than beer or flat soda.

Danny followed Beth to the deck and sat on a plastic chair while she went inside to get the drinks. He could hear her humming from the other side of the screen door as she fiddled around in the kitchen.

By this time the toddlers had noticed something different in their little world. They made their way up the steps, staring at Danny apprehensively. Danny was beginning to think that he'd made a mistake, as he really didn't want to make small talk with a couple of three year olds. He glared at them and growled under his breath. That was all it took, they were running back to the safety of their tree again. That was fine with Danny, but he knew enough from watching Sally growing up that they would be back. Toddlers are like kittens, Danny thought, the only difference being that you couldn't shove firecrackers up their asses.

"It's not much, but it's cold." The door banged open and Beth came out with two big tumblers filled with ice and lemonade. She offered one to Danny and took one cautious glance towards the children before slipping into the other plastic chair across from him.

Danny thanked her and took a large gulp of the tart liquid.

"I guess you *were* thirsty." Beth smiled.

They talked for a while about petty subjects, where they were from, why she moved there. To get away from her ex-boyfriend, she said. Danny was especially pleased that she didn't seem the least bit impressed that Nick was his stepfather. She actually said that she wouldn't watch his newscasts anymore after Danny told her what had happened. All except the masturbating part, that is. He really didn't even want to talk about that whole subject but when she asked about his swollen nose he didn't want to start changing his story this late in the game. He was well aware that in order to make a story believable you have to stick with it. Telling different people different versions almost always leads to confusion as to who you told what

to, which will lead to getting caught. No sir, Danny was too

smart for that.

Sitting back down with freshly refilled glasses, Beth

began telling Danny how much she loved art. Danny didn't

know shit about art or artists but was happy to listen to this

woman. Yes, woman. She pulled her tan legs up under her

and Danny could feel the stirring in his pants again.

"Is your dad an artist?" she asked.

His mind reluctantly climbed out from between her

thighs when she mentioned Jeff. "No, why?" He hoped she

wouldn't ask what it was that he did do. He could feel his

fingers start tapping on the arm of the chair but was

powerless to stop it.

"Oh, no reason. It's just that I spend a lot of time

out here with the kids and I noticed that he hangs out in his

shed quite often. So I figured he was a sculptor, or painter

or something. I figured that's why he put the air conditioner

in the shed. To keep the clay from getting too soft or the

paint from running in the heat. I guess I'm being nosy, and

don't take offense, but he seems to keep that shed in better

condition than his trailer." She took a sip from her glass

and they both looked up the road at his dad's property.

She's right, Danny thought. I wonder why I never

noticed it before. The shed has power going to it and Danny

noticed the air conditioner in one window. The trailer itself only had one old box fan to keep cool with. Also, the other window on the shed had dark, well kept curtains that were constantly drawn. The trailer, on the other hand didn't even have blinds. This stood out because Danny remembered having to nail a towel up over the bathroom window on his first visit, just so he could take a shit without the neighbors watching. Apparently privacy was more an issue in the shed than the shitter for Jeff, he thought.

"Do you need to use the bathroom? I noticed your fingers tapping over and over and thought you might have to pee."

"Oh," Danny fidgeted and crossed his arms over his chest, "no, I'm fine, it's just a habit I have. Well, thanks for the lemonade, but I guess I really should be going." He noticed the children were again on the approach, but that wasn't why he wanted to leave. No, he wanted to check something out. "It was nice meeting you, Beth." He stood up and pulled his shirt away from where the sweat had stuck it to his back.

"I enjoyed it too." She looked at him puzzled. "Did I offend you? If so, I didn't mean to. Sometimes my mouth has a way of running without my brain's help." She tapped the side of her head as if to say 'wake up in there'.

"No, you didn't offend me at all. You've just got me a little curious." He smiled at her. She looked kind of cute with that mock 'I'm brain dead' look she had given.

102

"Hell, maybe he is an artist. Maybe I'll find out."

As he turned to go she gently held his arm. "Let me know what you find out, OK?" Beth looked as excited as a bride on her wedding day.

"It's a deal." Danny waved and walked back up the street towards his dad's trailer. When he reached the steps of the deck he looked over towards the shed. That will have to wait, he thought.

He couldn't get Beth off of his mind at the moment. The way she looked hanging clothes, how she gently held his arm when he tried to leave. Man was she hot. Danny found himself on the toilet in the bathroom stroking himself for all it was worth. Imagining Beth laying in her yard, naked. Begging him to take her.

As he came, he called out her name through gritted teeth before slumping back against the water tank, exhausted.

Nick had been asleep on the couch for a few hours when he was awakened by Pam coming home with some groceries. He regretted his afternoon indulgence as he sat up and stretched.

"Need some help?" he asked his wife.

"No thanks, this is all of it." She nodded at the two bags in her arms.

Nick walked over and took them from her, leaning

over to kiss her cheek as he did.

"Rough day, Honey?" She wrinkled her nose as she smelled the alcohol on his breath.

"You could say that. Sit down. I'll share my whole world with you." Nick sighed.

Noticing how serious he looked, Pam became concerned. He couldn't know, she thought. Nick wasn't the kind of man to kiss her just before he accused her of fucking his best friend. "What's wrong?"

Nick set the groceries on the counter and absently dug through the bags. Coffee, cereal, assorted flavors of Kool-aid. She's still shopping as if the kids were here, he thought.

"Nick?" Pam was behind him now.

Nick pulled two bottles of soda from the refrigerator and opened them. Turning around, he handed one to Pam and began. "Ernie put me on hold this morning. I'm on suspension until I'm cleared of all the charges." He looked at his bottle until this bit of news took effect.

"What?" Pam stared in disbelief. "Is he an idiot? You were at the station when it happened." She set her drink on the table and shook her head. "After all the years you've been there, how can they even think...?"

"I know all that, Pam. It's business. Our advertisers are threatening to pull out. He says he knows I didn't do it, but other people are at stake here. Other jobs that people could lose if our advertisers desert us." He took a drink and pulled her to him. "I wish I knew what caused him to do all this."

Pam was confused. "Ernie? But you just said…"

"Not him." Nick slammed his drink down so hard that it started foaming over. "I understand why Ernie suspended me, even though I don't like it. What I don't understand is why Danny started all this shit!" Getting a rag from under the sink, he stopped mid-reach. "Has he ever done anything like this before?"

"What do you mean, before?" Pam directed.

Nick stood up and started wiping the puddle surrounding his bottle. "You know, before. When you were with Jeff. Any other psychotic outbursts?" He tossed the rag into the sink.

"Well, let me think, there was the homeless man that he pissed on when he was ten. Oh, and that time he stole a cripple's prosthetic arm." Pam said sarcastically. "Look Honey, I know what your job means to you, and I know you're upset. You have every right to be, but lashing out at me isn't going to change things. You lost your job, but I lost my children!"

Nick fell into a chair and stared at her. His ego battling with rational thought. This was his wife for crying out loud, not some bimbo he picked up in a bar. Too many people had been clouding his judgment with paranoid bullshit the past few days. People a hell of a lot less important to him than his wife. She was right, he thought. No matter how screwed up Danny was, he was still her son, her flesh and blood.

What about Sally? Who was the real victim here, anyway? An adult whose career was temporarily suspended, with pay to boot, or an innocent little girl who was yanked from her home and loving family without so much as an explanation?

Nick sat upright and let out a sigh. Reaching over to take his wife's hand he apologized.

"You're right, Honey," he whispered. "We need to stick together through this, not look at each other for places to lay blame. The important thing is for us to be there for Sally. This has got to be hard as hell on her. We need to comply with D.S.S. and jump through their hoops, as Ted says, and bring her home."

Pam was smiling at him as tears filled her eyes. How could she have been so wrong about him? When it came right down to it he did put the kids and her first, ahead of his career. She loved him so much at that moment that it overwhelmed her. Her tears had started to trickle down her cheeks dropping one by one onto the table.

"Pam?" Nick looked concerned. "Are you OK? What's wrong?"

Pam walked around the corner of the table and

106

leaned over, pulling him close. "I'm sorry too." She

sobbed. "I'd forgotten how much I love you."

"I love you too." Nick stood up, bringing her

clinging body upright. He put her wet cheeks in his hands.

"We'll get through this." He tried to reassure her. "My

priorities get a little out of whack sometimes. I don't know,

I guess I'm a little overwhelmed with all of this. You're

right though, we are together, and no damn social worker

with a God complex from The Department of Stupid

Shitheads is going to take that away from us."

Pam really felt like a piece of shit at that moment.

How could she have done this to him? Slept with Ted. Her

dad was right, she was a worthless whore. Pam just kept

thinking that over and over as Nick held her tight, stroking

her hair.

After a few minutes Pam's tears had stopped and

she was regaining her composure. Nick looked down at his

tear soaked shirt and smiled at her.

"Tell you what," He handed her a box of tissues

from the counter next to them. "Why don't you wipe your

eyes? I'll change my shirt and we'll go and see our

daughter."

Pam went numb. She couldn't face Ted. Not now.

Not after this. She would have to figure out a way to tell

him that it was over. She still loved Nick. She had to tell

him, but not now. Her emotions were in overdrive and

seeing him and Nick laughing and carrying on, knowing Ted had been inside her just a few short hours earlier, would be too much.

"How about this," she said, "Why don't you go over there and pick her up. We'll take her to dinner. Just the three of us. Meanwhile, I'll get ready. I imagine all my tears caused my mascara to turn me into an Alice Cooper look alike right now." She struggled up a smile.

"All right," Nick laughed, "let me throw on another shirt and I'm outta here, Alice."

After Nick left, Pam went into their bathroom and turned on the sink. She looked at the reflection of herself in the mirror as the water warmed up. Well dad, she thought, I bet you're finally proud of your little princess. How I finally lived up to your expectations.

"Fuck you!" She yelled and spat at the reflection. She watched the saliva make its long journey down the glass while her hands held a white knuckle grip on the edge of the counter. She didn't move until the steam from the water fogged up the image in front of her. "Fuck you." She whispered and began the process of changing from Alice Cooper back into the more civilized Pam Roanik.

Nick hadn't even opened his car door before Sally came flying off the Anders' porch screaming, "Daddy, Daddy!"

He stepped out and scooped her into his arms as Nora watched through the window.

"How's my little girl!" He hugged her. It felt to him that he hadn't seen her in weeks instead of the couple of days that it had been.

"I miss you and Mom. When can I come home?" She demanded as he kissed her cheek.

"Soon, baby girl, real soon." Nick hoped. Then when he tried to set her down, she would have no part of it. Nick ended up carrying her to the door to say hi to Nora.

"She's missed you."

"We've missed her, too." He looked into Sally's smiling face as he spoke. "Thanks so much for helping us, Nora, I owe you. Has she been any trouble?"

"Not one ounce. It's nice to have a child around for a change. Come inside."

Sally finally let Nick put her down and the two of them followed Nora into the kitchen.

"She's been keeping us both busy with all her art work." Nora said, pointing at the crayons covering a table surrounded by various drawings of dogs, cats, and horses.

"I have one here for you." Sally dug through the pile and finally found a drawing of a man sitting behind a desk that had a big number 11 on it. "This is you, Daddy, do you like it?"

"I love it, sweetheart. Thank you! It looks just like

me."

"I drew one of Mom and Danny, too." She said while digging through the pile again. When she found them Nick bragged on how close they looked like her mother and brother as well. Sally's face lit up even more.

Nora stood beside Nick smiling at the two of them. "Sometimes I regret our decision not to have kids." She sighed. "How's Pam holding up?"

"What? Oh, as well as can be expected." Nick told her, somewhat distracted. Looking at the picture of Danny, there was something that bothered him. He couldn't put his finger on it. Hell, it's probably just in my mind. A crayon drawing of Danny by a nine year old, what could it be? "I'm sorry, Nora," he folded the three pictures and put them in his pocket, "Pam's holding up, kind of depressed though. Well, you'd expect that. I was hoping we could take Sally with us for a few hours. Have dinner maybe, cheer us all up. Do you think that would be a problem?"

"I can't believe you're even asking me this, Nick." Nora shook her head. "Of course it's all right, she's your daughter."

"I'm coming with you?" Sally had resumed her coloring, but dropped her crayon when she overheard this.

"For a while, Sweetie. Do you want to go see your Mom?"

"You bet!" She started putting the crayons back in

their box. "And Danny, too!"

Nora and Nick looked at each other. "Well, it'll just be the three of us today, Sweetie." Nick forced a smile. I guess today would be as good a time as any to tell her about Danny, he thought. Not here, though. Not now. This would be something Pam and he would do together. Even though Sally was comfortable with the Anders' she's been through enough not to have her mother beside her while we tried to explain why her world has been torn apart.

"Danny isn't home either?" she asked.

"Help me get your pictures together, Sweetie, your Mom will want to see how pretty you draw." Nora diverted the question.

Nick was relieved. He made his living thinking on the spot and for the first time that he could remember, he couldn't think of a thing to say. He suddenly felt a pang of guilt for every story he'd done on families whose children were taken by D.S.S. Sure he justified that some of them were legitimate. Truly abused children that needed help, but how many others. How many families were separated by a cookie-cutter system that claimed to help? Nick remembered the thick glass and locks that separated the social workers from the people they supposedly help. That and the bullet hole. He wondered how many other innocent children right now were staying with friends, or in a foster home while D.S.S. ran their parents through a ring of fire.

Just because they've "done studies."

He was looking at one right now. One little girl who can't come home and doesn't even know why. Hell, Nick didn't even know why.

"All ready, Daddy." Sally smiled at him. "What's wrong? You look upset."

Nick didn't realize he was wearing his thoughts on his face. "Not a thing, Sweetie." He picked her up and gave her a hug. "I love you."

"I love you, too."

Nora smiled at them. She had seen Nick's face, too. She knew it was tearing him apart. In all the years she'd known him, she never once saw him treat Sally as anything less than his own real daughter. Danny too, for that matter. "You guys have a good time." She patted Nick's shoulder.

"Thanks. We won't be late." Nick told her as she walked them to the door.

"Now, don't worry about that. I'm sure D.S.S. and their little spies don't work past 5:00, so you won't have them to think about. Relax and enjoy yourselves. You deserve it. Isn't that right, Sally?" She tousled the little girl's hair.

"Let's go," was her reply.

Nick and Sally buckled into the SUV and backed out of the drive as Nora waved. She thought again about Ted and their decision not to have children. Maybe it was best. After all, it seemed to her, all the parents do anymore is make the babies. Then the government takes control of the family. Nora sighed and closed the door

----

"Mom, I'm home!" Sally burst through the front door and ran through the place looking for her mother.

"Boo!" Pam jumped from behind her bedroom door as Sally ran in.

"Aay!" she screamed. "You scared me!"

Pam got down on one knee and pulled her daughter into her arms. "I've missed you so much, Honey." She showered Sally with kisses.

"Me, too!" Sally kissed her back. "Dad said we could only spend the afternoon together. How come I can't stay here anymore? Did I do something wrong?"

Nick was standing in the hallway leaning against the doorjamb.

"No, Honey, of course you didn't do anything wrong." Pam kissed her forehead. "Your father and I have some things to take care of and we just thought you'd like to visit with Aunt Nora while we did them." She looked at Nick hopefully. "You're having fun over there aren't you?" Pam almost pleaded.

"I guess so, but their house always smells funny," Sally answered.

Nick laughed. "That's just the smell of Ted's pipe.

It kinda takes over the place, doesn't it?"

"It kinda stinks." Sally stated.

"Ah, the honesty of youth." Nick smiled.

"Are you two getting a divorce? Is that why you don't want me here?" Sally asked without missing a beat.

Pam felt a lump rise up in her throat. "Of course not, Honey, and we do want you here. Don't ever think otherwise. We're your family and we love you." She hugged her daughter again. "Tell you what, before you go back tonight, you can get some of your favorite toys to take with you. You don't want to be without your tiger, do you?" Pam was referring to Sally's favorite stuffed animal. A brown floppy cat.

"OK, then who's up for pizza!" Nick tried to lighten the mood.

"I am! I am!" Sally cheered.

"Then let's get going before they run out of pepperoni!" Nick kidded.

"Oh, Dad! You know we always get sausage." Sally teased back.

As the three of them started to leave, Sally stopped them. "Mom, Dad, can I ask you something?"

"Sure, Honey, anything." They both looked at her.

"Well, if I didn't do anything wrong," she paused, "and you're not getting a divorce," she looked at each of them, "then am I staying away because of the way Danny's

What Goes Around

been acting?"

by Mick Woodhall

CHAPTER V

Ann Randall was going over some files in her office. Over two weeks had passed since she was embarrassed by Ted Anders at the Roaniks' team meeting, but she was still angry. One thing Ms. Randall couldn't stand was to be humiliated. Which is just what Ted had done to her, on her territory, in front of her co-workers.

Okay, Mr. Big Shot lawyer, she thought, you may have won the battle regarding the little girl, for now. Ann had talked to the D.S.S. attorney about the temporary custody order and found it to be legally binding. You better enjoy her company, Ann's thoughts continued, because if I have my way she'll be graduating high school before your client's get her back.

She slammed the file cabinet shut with such force that it tilted back against the wall. Sitting down she took a deep breath and spread open the Roanik file. She knew how long these things can drag out. Hell, the boy would be an adult before his parents got half way done with the anger management classes alone. She smiled, knowing what a waste of time those classes were. Most of them were nothing more than group sessions, supervised by idealistic ex-hippies who run them to get ideas for some book they never end up writing. After all, who wants to read about some redneck that gets drunk and smacks around his wife or kid.

She couldn't believe the gall of the Roaniks. Ann thumbed through their file again. Trying to convince me that the boy hit himself. What do they think I am, an idiot? I've been working in child services too many years to fall for something like that. Ann was getting angry again. She stubbed out the cigarette she had just lit and stared at the pictures of Danny. "Yeah, he did that himself. Right," she said while examining the boy's nose. "Patty, get me Justine Woodward." Ann spoke into her intercom.

"Yes Ma'am," came Patty Strickend's static reply from the outer office.

Five minutes later, social worker Justine Woodward, was sitting opposite Ann in her office.

"Justine, you've had some time to go over this case now. Tell me what you think," began Ann.

"Well, we have a teen-age boy who's been in trouble with the law before and..." started Justine.

Ann bolted upright in her chair. "In trouble with the law? For what?"

"A couple of years ago he vandalized a television

117

station. Teen-age stuff, graffiti, some broken windows."

Ann hadn't heard about this. "What station?"

Justine thumbed through her notes, "Channel 11."

"Channel 11? Are you sure?" Ann came up out of her chair.

"Yes. Why?"

"Don't you see?" She grinned. "Nick Roanik works for Channel 11. Could you imagine his embarrassment having to tell them that it was his stepson that trashed the place?"

"That would be rough." Justine pondered.

"I imagine it would be rough enough on a man of Mr. Roaniks' stature that it could fester inside him for months. Even years. Eating away at him until he finally snaps." Ann was pacing as she spoke, another cigarette burning between her fingers. "I think it's about time for one of your surprise visits to the Roaniks' house, don't you?"

"I'll take care of it." Justine said as she prepared to leave.

"Keep me informed on every aspect of this case, Justine." Ann told her as she walked her to the door. After she closed it, Ann sat down at her desk and leaned back smiling. "Ted Anders, we have a motive. Let's see you worm your client out of this one," she muttered.

Back in her own office Justine sat down and opened her notes. It's almost 5:00, she thought. If she thinks I'm driving all the way out to their house from here without knowing if they're even home, she's wrong. That's almost thirty miles. She found the Roaniks' phone number and dialed. After six rings she hung up. I'll call them again in the morning. I'm not wasting my own time checking in on these people, she told herself.

With that, she got her purse and went home. After all, she thought, there's still several more days left in the month. It's not my fault that their lawyer made Ann Randall look like an amateur. Besides, that kid will be eighteen in less than a year and no longer her problem. Justine hated dealing with teenagers. She felt that most of them deserved a good ass-kicking anyway. What better person to do it than a loving parent, she thought.

All the time anymore with them it was, "give me this, you owe me that."

When she got in her kitchen she set her purse on the table and began to fix herself some coffee. Memories of the old days flooded her mind. It was Twenty-five years ago when she first started for D.S.S. She had become a social worker to be a voice for abused children. That's how it was back then. Social workers were taught to assess each individual case on its own merits, she remembered. Now they hand out the same list of classes and meetings to every family. Don't look at special circumstances, they say, our studies show that this way works.

Justine sat down at her table and set her coffee next to a partially completed jigsaw puzzle. She remembered all the times her dad took a switch to her legs when she was young. She hated it then, hated him, but never once did she call the police on him. Even if she had, she knew what they would say when they arrived.

"Mr. Woodward, what seems to be the problem?"

"Well, Red," her father had known all six police officers in their small town, "Justine snuck out of her window to meet up with that Thompson boy, so I whupped her."

"Is that true, Justine?" The cop would ask her.

"Yes Sir."

"Well, you seem to have it under control, Mr. Woodward. Now Justine, you can't be calling the police every time you go off and get into trouble at home. It's a parent's job to discipline their own children, not ours. "

Then he would make small talk with her dad, and when he finally left, her dad would bring out the switch again. This time for calling the police. Justine also knew that he would swing a lot harder this time, and with more swats to your legs. You wished you had never even heard of the police, much less called them. You knew you would never make that mistake again. If you did wrong you took your punishment, and that was that. That was how things were. Back then.

Justine picked up a puzzle piece and scanned over the section that looked like a sail. It was a scenic ocean view picture with some beach and docks and several boats.

How times have changed. Now, they not only had teenagers calling them every time they got grounded, but the damned school system was encouraging it. She remembered what started that mess. Kids were coming to school with bruises, and to keep from getting another beating from the bully who did it in the first place, they said the teachers hit them. Now every time a teacher sees a mark on a kid, they're so scared that they'll be blamed for it, they make the kids call us. Just thinking about this was making her angry.

Justine snapped the puzzle piece in place and took a sip of her coffee. All the time we waste sorting out these false claims, she thought, is time we should be devoting to helping the truly abused children out there. No sir. Justine Woodward did not like teenagers. It was just her luck, six months before she was due to retire, and she was assigned another one. To make matters worse, it was a family that her boss evidently wanted to see suffer. She smiled at the thought of that lawyer putting Ms. Randall in her place. Teenage boys play with themselves. It's normal, he had said. What a hoot!

Danny had waited long enough. The curiosity about

the shed was about to drive him nuts. He had searched the trailer for the key on the day he had lemonade with Beth and couldn't find it. That meant his dad had to have it on him.

Danny looked across the room at Jeff who had passed out in his chair again. A half full can of beer lie at his feet, draining onto the carpet. Danny had stopped taking them from his dad by this point. It didn't bother him at first or when he used to visit, but now that he had lived there for a while it had become annoying. After all, if his dad didn't mind a beer stained carpet, why should he?

Danny listened to his father's snoring for a minute before silently walking over. Jeff Nelson kept his keys on several extra large paper clips duct taped together hanging from his belt loop. Damn, thought Danny, it's a wonder he doesn't lose them. He reached between the arm of the chair and his dad's hip and felt for them. As he touched them his dad let out a loud fart and Danny pulled back. Listening to the unbroken sound of snoring, he relaxed a little and tried again. This time he was successful. His dad didn't even move.

There were four keys on the homemade key chain. He thumbed through them, examining each one. The brass one he knew belonged to the trailer and there was one that looked as if it would fit a riding lawn mower or something similar. Danny knew that the owner of the trailer park had a

riding mower and his dad sometimes mowed the
neighborhood for extra cash, so that was probably it.

He stole a glance over at his dad again. Still asleep.
Good. He turned his attention back to the keys and started
towards the door. There were still two more keys on the
clip that he couldn't identify. One of them had to be to the
shed. When he reached the door leading to the deck there
came a loud knocking from the other side. It startled Danny
and he dropped the keys on the floor with a clang.

"Huh, what, who the hell is it?" came Jeff's groggy
voice from behind Danny.

Danny turned to look at his dad and could tell that
although his eyes were open, he couldn't see through the
glassy, red orbs. Putting his foot on the keys, he told Jeff it
was nothing and to go back to sleep.

The knock came again and Jeff tried to work his
way out of the recliner. Danny thought he looked like
someone in an electric chair the way his arms kept shooting
forward, trying for something to grab a hold of. Finally he
gave up and passed out again. Danny let out a sigh of relief.
He bent down and picked up the keys, stuffing them into
the pocket of his jeans as he opened the door.

"Hi, Danny." It was Beth. "I haven't seen you in a
while and thought I'd stop by."

Danny looked back at his dad; made sure he was
still sleeping, and stepped out on the deck. After quietly

closing the door he turned back to Beth. "Shhh." He whispered, motioning with his finger as he led her into the yard.

"Sorry. I didn't know he was at home. Are you busy?"

"Uh, kind of." Danny remembered that she was the one that raised his interest in the shed in the first place, but he wasn't sure he wanted her to know what was in there. After all, it could be anything, and he hardly knew her.

"Oh," came her saddened reply. "I just got the kids to sleep and I thought you might like to go for a walk or something."

Danny looked at her and thought how pretty her face was in the moonlight. He didn't know what to think of her. Was she just bored and lonely, or was there something more. He decided it wouldn't hurt to let her look with him. What could his dad possibly have in there? Besides, he himself had been getting pretty bored lately. He didn't know anyone else in the area besides his dad's friends, and who wanted to hang out with a bunch of hicks, drinking beer and talking about hunting every night. He still didn't know how his dad could stand it.

"I um, have a better idea." He smiled at her and pulled the keys out of his pocket, holding them up for her to see.

Beth looked at the keys for a moment, then her eyes

lit up and she looked over towards the shed. "You don't think it will wake your dad, do you?" she asked.

Danny thought of his dad struggling to get conscious enough to get out of his recliner again. "We'll have to be quiet, but I think it'll be okay."

They walked together across the lawn to the shed. Danny inhaled the musky scent of sweat mixing with perfume as they stood together at the door.

"I feel like a kid at Christmas." She giggled.

As he slipped one of the keys into the lock, Danny thought that even though Beth was slightly older than he was, she did have a childish way about her.

"This one's not it," he told her when the first key didn't work. He held the keys up to the beam of the street light and looked for the other one he hadn't recognized. He selected it out of the group and slid it in the lock. His face fell when nothing happened.

"I don't understand?" He mumbled and tried the one that looked like a lawn mower key. No luck. Out of desperation he put in the trailer door key. "Damn," he said, looking at the lock in disbelief.

Suddenly a glow cast itself across the shed and they heard the sound of water splashing as Jeff relieved himself in the bathroom.

"Come on!" Danny unconsciously grabbed Beth's hand and they ran around the trailer and onto the next street. When they stopped by the row of mailboxes Danny realized he was still holding Beth's hand and let it go abruptly. "Sorry," he mumbled to her.

"Don't worry about it. I haven't had that much excitement in a long time." She smiled at him.

Danny turned red and changed the subject. "I don't understand it." He said again, looking at the keys. "I've looked everywhere. I could've sworn one of these would fit." He looked at her almost pleading. "Where else would he keep it?"

Beth couldn't help but laugh. "Have you thought of just asking him?" Danny couldn't tell if she was laughing at him or with him but either way he didn't much like it. Suddenly, the evenings silence was broken by the sound of his fingers tapping on the metal mail boxes.

"Don't you think if he wanted me to know what was in there; he wouldn't go to this length to keep it a secret?"

Beth looked at his hand and then his face, then back to his hand again. "Yeah, I guess you're right." No longer laughing. "Well, I need to go check on my kids. I'll see you around." She glanced at his hand still tapping away as he glared at her.

She gave a kind of half wave and started walking briskly towards her trailer. When she reached the door she looked back towards the mailboxes but Danny was gone.

Nick Roanik sat down in the semi-circle of men that made up his first anger management class. Just having to go there made him angry. He was one of about fifteen other guys who were required to attend one class per week for up to twenty-six weeks.

He looked around the room, and although the people looked like he expected, the class itself wasn't. Todd Suchland ran it more like an AA meeting than a class. Everyone took a turn telling about their week, how many people they hit, what their probation officer was up to, that sort of thing. The only thing that Nick felt he had in common with them was that as each person's turn came, they said at some point that D.S.S. was involved.

Nick wasn't naive enough to think that this band of drug users, alcoholics, and women beaters was innocent. What he did notice though, was that D.S.S. seemed to hand out the same list of crap to everyone.

Nick listened as a guy in an American flag headband was telling about how his girlfriend hit him across the head with a motorcycle helmet and when he grabbed it from her, she called the police. The man spent the night in jail on a domestic violence charge while she stayed home. The poor guy was trying to defend himself and now he lost his kid, has a record, and has to spend the next twenty-six Thursday evenings sharing his feelings with a bunch of strangers. The only thing that kept Nick from feeling sorry for him was that when he was released on bond, he went straight home and earned what he had been charged with. Todd didn't think that was too smart of him either.

Nick was also uncomfortable with the fact that even though everyone was strictly on a first name basis, he was known by the whole room. Some guy named George asked him if he was supposed to be there or if he was doing a report on anger management classes.

Nick told him that yes, he was required to attend but that didn't mean there wouldn't be a report in the near future on the abuse of power that is D.S.S. That got the whole room cheering.

Maybe this won't be so bad after all, thought Nick as they clapped, I can use all this to do an in depth story on D.S.S. and the lives they tear apart. He was definitely becoming biased to the negative side of the system.

As he told his story to the group, he couldn't believe himself how ridiculous it sounded. That pissed him off even more. It was hard to believe that a person would hit himself in the nose. After all, this wasn't Hollywood, and Danny wasn't Jim Carry trying to get out of a court date on Liar, Liar.

When Nick finished his story a man named Steve even asked him the same question he'd been hearing since the whole mess started.

"Did you see him hit himself, or is that what your wife told you? 'Cause my ex-wife is a lying cunt. She got stoned and fell over the dog. Then she told her probation officer that I put the marks on her to keep him from giving her a drug test."

Nick just shook his head. He was ready for them to move on to the next guy. He wondered what the women's' version of this would be like. Pam was scheduled to start her class the following Monday. He thought it would be funny if all the wives and girlfriends of his group would be in Pam's class. Then the two of them could have dinner afterwards and compare notes. He didn't think that would be likely though. That would be too convenient. D.S.S. does not make things convenient.

The Roaniks phone rang early the next morning. Pam set her coffee down and got up to answer it.

"Mrs. Roanik?" came the voice on the other end. "This is Justine Woodward. We met at the D.S.S. office a couple of weeks ago. How are you?"

"I'm fine," Pam looked over at Nick who was finishing his breakfast, "and you?"

"Fine. Thanks. The reason I'm calling is because I'll need to come out to your house today. How does 1:00 sound?"

"Hold on a second." Pam covered the mouth piece

and told Nick who it was.

"What does she want?" Nick scowled.

"To nose around in our lives. What else?" Pam said.

Nick shook his head in disgust and made a pumping motion with his fist.

Pam smiled. "1:00 will be fine," she said back in the phone.

"Very good, I'll see you then," Justine replied before hanging up.

Pam replaced the receiver and sat back down across from Nick. "How long is this going to last?" she wondered out loud while sipping her coffee.

"Well, Honey, Ted did tell us that this could take some time," said Nick.

Pam inadvertently flinched when he mentioned Ted. Hoping her husband didn't notice, she went on. "Haven't they done enough? Sally is living somewhere else, afraid we're divorcing, and God knows what's going on with Danny over there at Jeff's."

This time it was Nick's turn to flinch. He was really starting to hate hearing Danny's name.

"Nick? Can I ask you something?"

Nick put down his cup and looked at his wife. "Anything."

"I know that we're going through hell. I also know there's more to come, and that Danny is responsible for a lot of it." She paused and looked at her husband, downhearted. "I guess what I'm asking you is, do you hate him?"

Nick thought for a moment. Responsible for a lot of it? Hell, try all of it. He looked at his wife's hopeful face. "No, I don't hate him," he reassured her, "but I do have to say that I don't like him very much right now."

Pam could accept that. Although Danny was her son and she loved him, she couldn't honestly say that she liked him at the moment either.

"Well, let's get ready." Nick walked over and put his hand out to help his wife up. "We've got company coming."

At 12:45 the doorbell rang. Nick turned the television off and got up to answer it. After he looked through the peephole he turned to his wife and made the same pumping motion with his fist again. Pam laughed, knowing full well Justine Woodward was on the other side of the front door.

"Hello, Ms. Woodward." Nick greeted her with his T.V. smile. "Please come in."

"Thank you, and please call me Justine." She made her way past Nick and sat down in a chair opposite Pam. "Good afternoon, Mrs. Roanik."

"It's Pam. Can I get you something? Coffee?" Pam remembered her little joke the first time D.S.S. came over and stopped there.

"A glass of ice water would be nice, thank you." Justine replied.

Pam started to get up but Nick, who hadn't sat back down yet, stopped her. "I'll get it, Honey." He told his wife from his spot outside of Justine's field of vision. "Would you like something while I'm at it? Lemonade?" he asked Pam before silently mouthing the word 'martini' for her to see.

Pam covered her mouth to keep from laughing. "Lemonade will be fine." she told him.

"What I want to discuss with you folks today," began Justine after Nick handed her the glass and sat down next to his wife, "is the progress that you two are making on your requirements. Have you started anger management sessions yet?"

"I go on Thursday nights and Pam starts on Monday," came Nick's reply.

"Very good. What about your parenting classes?"

"Wednesdays. We go together," Pam told her.

Justine was taking notes as she spoke. "You've had other problems out of Danny over the years, is that true?" She asked Nick.

"Yes, I guess so." Nick was guarded. He didn't know what she was getting at.

"It's our understanding that two years ago, Danny

vandalized your place of employment."

Nick looked at Pam. He knew now that they weren't looking to help the family, they were looking for a motive. Anything they could use to win their case. He wasn't about to play that game. "Yes, yes he did. We discussed it and felt that he was lashing out. We thought that he might have been having feelings of resentment regarding Pam's divorce from his father. That's when we took him to see a psychologist." Nick told her.

Justine wrote for a minute then looked up at Nick. "How do the two of you get along?" she asked.

"Danny and I, or Pam and I?" Nick questioned.

"You and your wife. How often do you argue?"

"I don't see where that would be any of D.S.S. business, but I'd say I can count on one hand how many arguments we've had in the past year. Why?"

"I'll be honest with you." Justine set her pen and notebook down and looked directly at Nick. "I'm wondering why you're still here," Justine answered.

"Here? What do you mean?" Nick was confused.

"I'm sure your lawyer has told you. If the two of you were to get a divorce, you wouldn't have to attend the meetings and classes. For that matter, be a part of any of this. As a step-parent you have no ties to these children other than marriage to their mother."

Nick looked at Pam, shocked. "Wait a minute. First

your boss tells me that because I'm a step-parent, all of this

is my fault. Now you're telling me that if I desert my

family when they need me the most that I won't have to

play your reindeer games? What kind of people are you?

Does D.S.S. use families' lives as their personal chess

pieces? Who can we break up? Who can we drive over the

edge? Well, I have news for you, and your boss. I have no

intention of divorcing my wife for any reason, least of all to

avoid jumping through your hoops. As for having no ties to

these kids, I'm here to tell you that I've been more of a

father to them than that necrophiliac you sent Danny to live

with." Nick was irate. D.S.S. has done studies all right,

studies on how to piss people off. He thought.

Justine hadn't stopped writing in her notebook

throughout Nick's tirade. She finally set her pen down and

shook the cramp out of her hand. "I must say on a personal

note," she spoke to Pam, "You're very lucky to have him."

She pointed at Nick. "I've dealt with so many cases

involving step-parents and I can count on one hand," she

looked at Nick, "the amount of those couples that stayed

together through the whole process."

"Maybe that's a sign that you need to change the

process." Pam said, "And thank you, I am lucky to have

him." I realize that now, she thought.

"Maybe you're right." Justine sighed. "Well, that's

all I have for today, thank you for your time. I'll call you if

I need more, otherwise I'll see you next month." Justine
stood up to leave.

"Justine," Pam stood up. "Have you been out to see
Danny?"

"That's my next stop."

"Would you tell him that we love him?" Pam's eyes
started to water.

"Yes, I will. Thank you again."

Nick walked her to the door and after he closed it he
turned to give Pam the pumping fist again, but thought
better of it. His wife had let her tears flow.

"Did you mean what you said," she sobbed, "about
not leaving us, no matter what?"

Nick walked over and hugged her. "Of course I
meant it, Honey. I married you till death do us part, not till
D.S.S. do part us."

Pam held him tighter and rested her head against his
chest, thinking, this is the man I love. How could I ever
have gotten so separated from that? How could I ever have
done this to him? Ted. God, how could I ever have been so
stupid?

Justine arrived at Jeff's trailer at about 3:30. Jeff
had just finished mowing some lawns and was not pleased
to have to wait any longer for his afternoon beer. He was
smart enough not to drink one in front of the social worker,

135

but he felt it was his right to have a beer or twelve in his own home whenever he damned well felt like it. He decided to be gentlemanly and compromise on the issue. While Justine sat in the kitchen and talked to Danny, Jeff excused himself and went into the bathroom. Reaching into the cabinet, past the towels and stack of porn magazines, he felt around for what he knew would be there.

"Ah! In case of emergency, pour glass!" he whispered as his hand found the bottle. "Desperate times mean desperate measures!" He opened the pint of Jack Daniel's and, ignoring the whole concept of sipping whiskey, turned it up. "That's better," he said after swallowing the second gulp. He carefully placed the bottle back and reached for the mouthwash. No one tells Jeff Nelson what he can do in his own home, he thought as he swished the mint liquid around in his mouth.

After a minute he leaned over the sink to spit, thought better of it and swallowed the foamy substance instead. A prostitute had once told him, "Why spit it out when you can swallow it. Ten dollars, please." The last part of that didn't apply in this case, but the rest of it made sense.

A couple of years earlier Jeff had done a month in the county jail for stalking one of the cashiers at the Foodmart. A charge Jeff felt was totally unjustified. After all, he would tell people, how could it be stalking when she wanted me? During his stay, a cell mate had introduced him to the wonders of drinking mouthwash. Jeff didn't like it much at first, but he had to admit, it did make the month go by faster. As an added bonus, no one ever accused him of having less than pleasant breath. Since his release, he only had to resort to it in the lowest of times.

While Jeff was reflecting on his fresh breath, Justine was getting visibly irritated with Danny.

"Look Danny, for the third time," she sighed, "you don't live there now. I just can't drop you off and let you go in their house. If you'll give me a list of the things you want, I'll be happy to call your mom and have her pack them up and I'll bring them out on my next visit."

"Okay," said Danny, "but wouldn't it be less of a problem if you would just drop me off and let me go in to get what I need?"

Justine sat for a moment and watched Danny tap on the table. "I'm afraid I can't do that, Danny."

Danny looked at her angrily. "Why not? It's my stuff. I want it!"

"I have explained four times now. Let's move on. You can give me the list or not. It's up to you."

"I'm sorry, Justine. I've just been through so much. I'm afraid of what my mom will do with my things if she finds out how important they are to me. After all, she chose staying with Nick over keeping our family together."

137

Danny's tapping continued. Clearly this woman wasn't understanding him. "You're supposed to protect me from them. So when you take me over there, make sure they're not around, okay? I have a key."

Justine shook her head in disbelief. She couldn't believe how close she was to smacking this kid herself. "I'm not taking you over there."

"But I need my stuff."

"Give me a list. End of discussion!"

Danny thought for a moment. "All right, but I can't remember exactly where everything is and I know you're a busy woman, so I don't want to waste your valuable time. I guess I'll just go with you so you won't have to reschedule any of your appointments." Danny nodded to himself as if to say the matter is now settled.

"That won't be necessary, but thank you for thinking of me, and my valuable time." Justine glared at him. He better have O.C.D., she thought, otherwise he was the biggest pain in the ass she'd ever dealt with.

Justine sighed with relief when Jeff came back before Danny could circle around again.

Jeff sat down opposite Justine. "Everything going okay?" He asked.

"Fine," Justine answered.

"Great, Dad." Danny smiled. His tapping had stopped now, which Justine took as a good sign. "You know, Dad," began Danny, "it gets pretty boring around here during the day while you work. I was wondering if you'd let Justine take me over to my friend Stans' house to hang out one day? There's no one here my age."

Jeff thought for a moment. "Where does Stan live?"

"A couple of streets over from mom's house. I haven't seen any of my friends since this happened. Please."

"Well, I'm sure Justine has other things to do. I don't think it's her job to be a chauffeur. What do you think, Justine?"

I can't believe the gall of this kid. Justine told herself. Does he think I'm an idiot? "I'm afraid not, Mr. Nelson. It's not a good idea." She smiled at Danny.

"Well, I guess I can call that Randall lady. She'll find someone to take me," was Danny's reply.

Fine with me, thought Justine. Then, totally ignoring Danny's attempt at a threat, she turned to Jeff. "As you know, it could be a while before Danny is returned to his mother, if at all. After all, he's almost an adult now." She glanced at Danny's reaction to this. Seeing there was none, she continued with Jeff. "What plans are you making regarding his license, a job, getting him registered in his new school, and so on?"

"Well," Jeff considered this. "Since he's almost an adult, wouldn't those be his concerns?"

"Mr. Nelson," Justine was shocked, "by law Danny doesn't become a legal adult until he turns eighteen. Since he is not that age yet, then as his father it is your responsibility to care for him. If you're not up to that task then perhaps we should look at different placement options."

"What are you saying?" Jeff stood up. "That I'm not a good father? I'm not the one that ran off with the abusive reporter! I didn't bust him in the nose! Everything was fine before. Pam did this to us. To him. It's all her fault. Her and that... Nick!"

"Sit down Dad, there's no reason to get upset." Danny had been watching Justine's pencil flying across her note book as Jeff talked. He wasn't pleased with the look on her face, either. The last thing he wanted was to be moved to some group home full of bed wetters and losers. He would have to handle it. After all, Justine was just a woman.

"Justine," Danny started, "I know that even though I live here, I'm in D.S.S. custody. I feel that I'm old enough to make my own decisions about my life. I mean, I'll be eighteen in December so that gives me plenty of time to prepare for my future."

"You think that roughly six months is enough time to prepare for your whole life?" Justine interrupted. "What exactly is your plan, Danny?"

"Well, I figured that since my grades are good enough, I could drop out of school and get my G.E.D., that way I could go to a community college at night and work during the day."

"That's your plan? Drop out of high school to go to college?" Justine asked.

"Sure. I already took all the senior courses when I was a junior, so now I can get a head start on college. Another year of high school would just waste my time."

Justine now thought she'd heard everything. "I don't think finishing high school would be a waste of time, Danny." Justine sighed. "You could graduate and still work in the evenings while you're a senior."

"That won't work. The evenings are for my time," was Danny's response.

Now Justine was confused. "I thought you said you would go to college in the evening? How is that your time?"

"I'd have to go to college at night because I'd be working during the day."

"So you're willing to give up your evenings for college but not for a job. Is that what you're telling us?"

Danny's fingers started their dance again. He thought he was being perfectly clear about this. Was she stupid? "I need to drop out of high school and get a job so I can go to college at night." He was getting frustrated.

Justine saw his fingers and knew where this was going. Circles again. In the little time she'd known Danny, she had realized that when he got an idea in his head it was staying put. No amount of common sense or reasoning would get through. She looked at her watch. It was almost 5:00. She had no intention of spending the evening, her time, going in circles with this kid.

"Dropping out is not an option." Justine said, firmly.

Danny was getting pretty sick of Justine telling him what he could and couldn't do. "If my dad signs the papers I can," he said defiantly.

"Nope. Sorry. I thought you understood. You live here, but you're in our custody, and D.S.S. isn't in the habit of letting their wards drop out of school. Here's a thought, though. If you're so determined to go to school at night, we could transfer you to night classes at the learning center. It's where most drop-outs go after they realize their mistake and want to get their lives back in order."

Danny glared at her. "I don't want to drop out because I'm stupid! Look at my grades! I want to drop out to better myself. I'm not going to some second chance school for pregnant teens and dope heads."

"Well then, I guess we have one other option." Justine collected her things and stood up. "You'll just have to finish your senior year and get a job on 'your time'."

Danny was tapping his routine with both hands now. O.C.D. in stereo. "I guess it wouldn't hurt anything if I asked the Judge when we go to court."

"You do that. Mr. Nelson, thank you for your time." She thought about telling him to call if he needed any thing but decided against it. No, she thought, it would be better to deal with Danny as little as necessary.

Jeff stood up and shook her hand. He was ready for her to leave as well. It was well past 'Miller time' and he was getting a headache. "Thank you, Justine. When will we see you again?"

"Some time next month. Unless we get a court date sooner. I'll let you know."

Justine told Danny good-bye and walked out. She racked her brain when she got into her car and couldn't for the life of her remember another kid that annoyed her as much as Danny. She backed out of the gravel driveway while thinking of how obsessed Ann Randall was with this case. It doesn't surprise me, she told herself, she and the boy are both crazy.

CHAPTER VI

Later that evening, things were calm in the Nelson home. Jeff was passed out as usual and Danny sat on the couch thinking about the social worker's visit. She is definitely going to be a problem, he told himself. He knew he had to handle her carefully though. Danny cursed himself that he hadn't even considered the possibility of a group home when he started this. That would be unacceptable. He had things just where he wanted them for now. Sure, the lack of edible food was getting old, but other than that his plan was going very smooth.

Danny looked over at his dad. He couldn't believe it. A dark stain was spreading across the front of Jeff's jeans. What has happened to you, Dad? he thought. How could you let that bitch ruin you? Danny felt sorry for his father, but the longer he lived with Jeff the more he felt a different emotion. Disgust. He turned away from his dad and flipped on the TV. It's like he won't even try to get his act together, Danny thought.

The sound of the television woke Jeff. He looked around for a second, then shivered. "Did I spill something?" He slurred when he saw his pants.

"Yeah, Dad." Danny answered, then thought, your bladder.

Jeff seemed okay with the response and fell back asleep.

Danny had had enough. He flipped the TV off again and stood up. He wondered what Beth was doing. He saw from the clock in the kitchen that it was only 9:30 so she was probably still awake. Danny walked to the bathroom thinking that he might go see her. He opened the cabinet and as he reached for his comb his arm knocked over the whiskey bottle that his dad had neglected to hide earlier. Looking at it he wondered if there was any place his dad didn't drink. Danny stood the bottle back upright and noticed the stack of magazines. Like any teenage boy would, he picked them up and sat on the closed toilet to thumb through them. He fought the urge to touch himself as he methodically admired each model. His erection was pounding as he got farther and farther through the pile. Danny was about to give in to it by the time he reached the final magazine. However, all thoughts of making mental love to one of the previous beauties left him when he opened its cover.

Much to Danny's confusion, inside the cover was not another batch of the naked babes he had been expecting. No, the magazine itself was missing and in its place was a neatly folded newspaper. Yellowed with age but otherwise well preserved in plastic wrap. The headline staring back at him rang through Danny's mind. 'Local mortician arrested for necrophilia'.

Why would he want to keep this, he thought, and why here? In a stack of fuck books?

Danny picked up the paper and felt the stiffness of it. Jeff Nelson, owner of Nelsons Funeral Home was arrested at his place of business yesterday after a continuing investigation, Danny read.

He began to feel light headed. Danny certainly didn't want a memento of all the lies his mother told to get his dad in this trouble, so why would Jeff?

When he got to the bottom of the article he saw it was continued on page A-7. Not wanting to go on, but unable not to, he slowly opened the paper. Careful not to tear the aged item, he turned it page by page instead of flipping through it all at once. His anger at his mother swelled again. Dad was good to us. Why did she have to start all those rumors that lead to this? he thought.

His father had told him why of course. She had been having an affair with Nick and wanted to make sure Jeff would be out of the picture so the two of them could be

146

together. He remembered his father's hurt laugh when he told Danny how shocked Pam looked when they dismissed the charges. That was when, Jeff had told him, he knew she was responsible. Danny believed every bit of it. After all, this was his dad, and Pam *was* with Nick.

Before Danny could calm down enough to finish finding the page, a knock on the bathroom door startled him. In his haste to put everything back in place Danny barely noticed the key that fell out of the folds of the newspaper. He quickly put everything back in order and into the cabinet while his dad mumbled something through the door about having to take a shit.

"Damn," Danny grumbled, his fingers tapping on the sink. "Why can't he just shit in his pants, then the back would match the front."

Danny looked around the bathroom and was about to let his dad in when he saw it. A brass key lying in the middle of a group of dried piss stains in front of the toilet.

"Hurry up in there, I've got to go!" Jeff's pounding on the door got Danny moving again.

"Almost done, Dad." Danny stalled while picking up the key with a wad of toilet paper. He then flushed the toilet for effect and opened the door for his dad to stagger in. He almost knocked Jeff over in his rush to get to the kitchen. Danny was willing to bet he knew what that key would unlock, but that would have to wait. The key had landed in piss, and dried or not, Danny didn't like touching it. He washed both his hands and the key several times while his dad was in the bathroom.

When he heard the toilet flush, Danny jammed the key deep in his pocket. He would have to wait until his dad either left or went back to sleep to test the key in the shed door. That was okay with Danny. He also had to figure out a way to get to his mom's house. There was something there he desperately needed. He would use the time he had to wait trying to solve that problem. He patted the key through his pocket and thought of Beth. By the way, he thought, does she have a car? He couldn't remember if he'd seen one at her trailer before.

Pam and Nick were lying beside each other, exhausted. The whole mess was taking a toll on them both as a couple and as individuals. Nick had really come to despise Danny. Of course he couldn't tell his wife that. Hearing something like that from her husband would tear her heart out. Hell, Nick hated himself for feeling that way but he couldn't help it. Everybody had tried every way they could think of to get the kid help for his issues, and how does he thank them? Why, in one selfish act he tears apart the whole family, that's how. Nick took a few breaths to calm down. He didn't want to wake Pam. He couldn't figure it out. All of this just to move to his dad's? Nick

148

thought about this. There has to be more to it than that.

He looked over at Pam's sleeping form. What about her? I know this has put a strain on her, he thought. She's been acting differently lately. Distant one minute, then clinging to him the next. Not at all like the strong woman he had fallen in love with. No, something more than this mess is on her mind. Nick had more questions than answers and he didn't like it.

Nick laced his hands behind his head and stared at the ceiling of their dark bedroom. He told himself it was time he did a little Charlie Tibbens style work of his own. There was more going on here then a boy wanting his daddy and Nick was going to find out what it was. After all, he was a reporter, and that's not much different than a detective, right? We both sort through the shit to find the facts, he told himself.

Trying not to disturb his wife, Nick slid out of bed and went down the hall into Danny's room. Closing the door behind him, Nick scolded himself for not thinking of this sooner. The key to this was that damn vase. It wasn't in the living room when Nick got home that night, so where was it? He suspected it was somewhere in this room.

He walked over to Dannys' dresser and began to wonder if it really mattered. He opened the top drawer and sifted through his stepson's clothes while thinking that even if he could produce the vase, that Olsen-Randall woman wouldn't believe him anyway. He could see her reaction in his mind, "You went to the store and bought another one, didn't you Laura Ingalls?"

Picturing this did not deter him. I need to find this vase for me, he told himself, to stop these doubts about Pam.

Even as he finished with the last drawer he struggled with the truth about that night. Damn that Charlie Tibbens! he thought. The whole thing was confusing him.

Nick continued his search. The night stand, under the bed. Even behind the posters on Danny's wall. A grasp, yes, he thought, but Nick had seen 'The Shawshank Redemption'. Leave no stone unturned, he reminded himself, heading for the closet.

He opened the door and stood back, taking in the contents. "Talk about an O.C.D. case study." He whistled. Nick had never seen a teenager's closet so neat and organized. Hell, he had never seen a teenager's *anything* so neat and organized. The top shelf had a row of shoe boxes with a typewritten index card taped to the front of each, listing their contents in alphabetical order. Video games, CD's, also all alphabetized.

Nick looked through each box slowly and laughed quietly as an idea struck him. He took a box of compact discs off of the shelf and set it on Danny's bed. One by one he opened them and put a different one in each case. Then he put the whole stack back in the box in an entirely different order. Smiling, he put the box back on the shelf and as a final touch he turned it so that the index card was facing the wall.

"You know, that was pretty childish."

Nick jumped as Pam's voice took away his fun.

"I didn't hear you come in. Did I wake you?" Nick asked.

"No, I had a bad dream." She walked over and hugged him. "What were you doing?"

"Looking for something." Nick replied.

Pam looked around her son's room thoughtfully. "The vase?"

"Yes."

"I looked through here all ready. Not as thoroughly as you though." She glanced at the misplaced shoe box.

Nick gave her a sheepish grin. "Tension breaker."

Pam sighed. "Any luck?"

Nick shook his head. "I've turned this room upside down and I can't find it. Where could it be?" He caught his tone being almost accusing as he asked the last part.

Pam shrugged. "I wish I knew."

"Well, let's go back to bed," Nick stretched, "I need to let this go for awhile."

Nick wasn't able to let it go for long. The following night was their parenting class. Nick and Pam were glad that at least they were allowed to face this part together.

They weren't sure what to expect when they arrived at the

building where the class was being held.

When they pulled into the parking lot they saw

several other couples already there. Some were in groups,

laughing and smoking. Others stood by themselves, looking

nervous. All were younger than them.

"Well," Nick scoffed, "Let's go learn how to build a

better parent." He took Pam's hand and led her to the door.

When they got to the room where the class was held

the door was still locked. Pam looked at her watch. "I

wonder if their going to show us how to teach our kids

punctuality?" she said as a woman came rushing through

the building's side entrance apologizing.

"I'm sorry I'm late. I had a class that ran long." The

woman said, unlocking the door.

Everyone filed into the room behind the woman and

found a seat at one of the tables. The tables that were set up

in almost the same way as the ones at the D.S.S. meeting,

Nick noticed. The Roaniks' were grateful to find a seat in

the back corner. Neither of them was in the mood for the

forced participation that they figured would be a part of the

class. Blend into the crowd, they both thought. The crowd

of twenty-somethings and teenage parents that is.

"Hello, my name is Elaine Finkmeyer," began the

woman when everyone was seated. "Welcome to Parenting

class. I'm glad you all could make it. I'll start by passing
around this sign-in sheet. Please make sure you print your
name clearly so you can receive proper credit for attending
each week. It is very important that you attend all ten
classes. I'm required to report all absences to your case
worker, and missing more than one session will require you
to take the whole class again." By this time the sign-in
sheet had made it around the room of about sixteen people
and back to her. Elaine picked it up and verified the amount
of signatures to people. Nodding her head and seeming
pleased that everyone could write their names, she passed
out name tags. "Very well," she said after everyone was
properly identifiable, "what we're going to work on over
the next ten weeks is a foundation to help each of you deal
in a healthy manner the day to day issues of being a
responsible parent. The subjects that we'll be covering will
help you in dealing with the stressful situations you may
encounter with your children in a positive, non-violent
manner. This class is very informative but you'll only get
out of it what you put in. I personally believe it would
benefit all new and existing families. Now, any questions?
Yes, Rhonda?"

Everyone looked toward the young woman with her
hand raised.

"Hi everyone, I'm Rhonda," she started. "Ms.
Finkmeyer, how long has this class been available?"

"Please everyone, call me Elaine. Let's try to keep this structured but informal. Through various funding and grants, programs like this have been in place for a number of years."

"I'm twenty-three years old and have four young children by myself. I mean, I have a boyfriend but he's not their father." Rhonda continued. "I've had problems with my kids before and have tried to get some kind of help like this but everyone told me that to take this class D.S.S. had to refer you. Why is that?"

"Well, Rhonda, that's not exactly true. There are a number of parenting classes through the private sector that are available to anyone for a fee. This, however, is one of the few that is state funded so it requires social service involvement to attend."

"How much is the fee for the other ones?" asked another young woman.

"It varies," Elaine answered, "Usually between one hundred and one hundred fifty dollars per session."

"Well if this class is so helpful," Rhonda again, "Then how come it's not affordable to the people who need it most? I don't know about anyone else's situation here, but as a single mother it takes every penny I earn just to feed, clothe, and put a roof over my kids' heads. It's hard enough just to make ends meet, and when I got overwhelmed I went looking for help. Wouldn't my taking this class, have better suited me and my children before the situation got so bad that my kids are now in foster care?" She was crying.

Elaine handed her one of the boxes of tissues from the desk in front. "I don't have any control over that, Rhonda. Look at it this way, when you do get your children back, you'll have the skills needed to better handle situations with them."

Pam couldn't believe what she was hearing. "How can this woman be so insensitive?" she whispered to Nick.

Nick was shocked as well. He raised his hand next. Elaine looked at him, relieved for the distraction.

"Yes, Nick?" She read his name tag.

"I was wondering, since this class is so important to D.S.S., and it obviously is since you say that's the only way we could all be here, are they required to take the class as a job requirement?" All eyes were on Nick and he heard whispering as some of the people began to recognize him.

Elaine was getting frustrated at the way this session was going. There was a lot of material to cover and they needed to move along. "No, they're not."

The class started murmuring and Nick and Pam looked at each other in disbelief.

"All right," Elaine took control again, "Let's move on."

That first class mostly covered new parents with

issues involving babies and toddlers. Nick and Pam began to feel even more out of place as it became clear that they were the only parents there with issues involving a teenager. In fact, they were the only parents there that even had a teenager. The average age of the children the other parents had was six years old. The oldest one being just nine. Pam was really beginning to wonder why they were even there.

"Elaine?" she interrupted. "I can see where this is helpful information for these young parents just starting out, but our problem is with a teenager. Will this class be covering anything beyond the terrible twos and elementary school issues?"

"Yes, definitely, Pam." Elaine got excited. "The last few weeks of class are designed to help parents with the confusing middle school years."

"Well I'm sure that will be a benefit to the parents in this room whose children haven't passed that stage yet. My husband and I were ordered here because of problems with my seventeen year old son. Seventeen and a half to be exact. What part of this class will assist us in dealing with him?"

"Well," Elaine had hoped there would be no more questions like these, "This class really doesn't deal very much with that age group, but the knowledge and skills you take with you from here will prove invaluable should you decide to have more children. Don't you think?" She smiled.

"My tubes are tied." Pam said flatly.

Although everyone except Elaine laughed at Pam's comment, both Pam and Nick were getting pretty disgusted at what they both felt was a waste of time in their case. Elaine had said it herself. The class doesn't go into much detail on dealing with someone six months away from adulthood. They left after that first session more frustrated than ever.

"Finally," said Danny when he saw Beth pull into her driveway. He had now been trying to see her for two days and his anxiety level was at an all time high. He jumped off of the deck and started walking towards her trailer. Beth noticed him coming and when she saw the intensity in his eyes she started to get uneasy. She remembered the last time she saw that look on him. Danny saw her face change when she saw him and knew he had better relax. He also remembered the way she hurried off the night at the mailboxes. Danny needed something from her so he didn't want to scare her off again.

"Hi Beth." He smiled when he caught up to her. "Need some help?" Danny pointed at the grocery bags in the open hatchback of her Escort. The one he now remembered seeing before.

"Sure," she said, warily. "Thanks."

Danny reached in the car and pulled out two of the bags and handed one to Beth before getting the third one. "Where are your kids?" he asked.

"They're spending a couple weeks with my mother," she said.

Beth led the two of them into her trailer and told Danny to put the bags on the table in the kitchen. She saw that his eyes no longer had that look to them and she let out a sigh of relief. He was a nice guy, she thought, but she saw something about him the night at the mailboxes that disturbed her. She couldn't put her finger on it but it was there none the less.

"You have a nice place here." Danny was putting on all his charm.

"Thanks." Beth answered as she put away her groceries. "That's right. You've never been inside here before."

"No, but I can mark it off my list of places I'd like to see the inside of now. Let's see, that just leaves a strip club and, well, my dad's shed." He smiled.

Beth laughed. "Well the way things are looking, you might just have an easier time getting into a strip club than that shed. Still no luck, huh?"

"No. I'm not giving up though. I found another key that might work but he hasn't left the trailer since then. Just the fact that he goes to so much effort to make sure no one gets in makes me that much more curious."

Beth offered Danny a chair and then sat down across from him at the table. "Is that why you were so worked up earlier?" she asked him.

"What do you mean?"

"Well, when you were coming over here you looked pretty, I don't know, determined about something. Was that it?"

"What? No. Actually," Danny stared at the table, "I kind of wanted to ask you a favor. It's kind of important." His eyes glanced up at her hopefully.

Beth couldn't help but smile at him. "Is that all? The way you looked I thought you were out to get someone." She laughed. "What's the favor?"

Danny had been working on a story to tell Beth for the whole two days he waited on her to come home. He had even forgotten about the newspaper article in the bathroom while he thought about it. He knew he couldn't just come out and tell her that he needed her to drive him to break into his mom's house. She would never go for that.

"I need to go talk to my mom. Check on her. Make sure she's all right. You know, her being there with Nick, alone. It worries me."

Beth looked at him with empathy. "That is so sweet of you, to care that much for your mother, bless your heart.

How can I help?"

Danny hoped he successfully hid his distaste at her comment. "Well, I need to go over there when Nick isn't around, you know, so she'll be more open with me. Not so afraid. I was really hoping you could give me a ride. It's just on the other side of town."

Beth thought for a moment. "I don't see why I can't do that for you. If I said no and then that pig did something to your mom, I couldn't live with myself. When do you want to go?"

Danny knew he had a short window where neither of them was likely to be home. Pam wouldn't be a problem. She was at her office until 5:00 all week. Nick would be the wild card. If he's doing a story in the area he sometimes drops by the house for lunch or something. Danny knew though, that from 3:00 on, Nick has to be at the station preparing for his newscast. His window for that day was all ready lost.

"How about tomorrow at 3:30?" he asked.

"I'm sorry, I can't do it then. I have a class on Fridays. I'm free Saturday though. Will that work?"

Saturday? How stupid is this woman? Danny thought. Nick does the news during the week. He's home on Saturdays. Dumb bitch. He could feel his fingers had begun their tapping ritual on his leg and was grateful that the table was there to block her view. He had to stay calm.

He needed her. She may be stupid, he thought, but stupid with a car.

"Danny?" She thought she saw a flicker of that something in his eyes again. "Is Saturday all right?"

Danny shook his head. "No. Nick doesn't work on the weekends." He hoped he didn't sound patronizing. "Are you free on Monday at the same time?"

"Monday's good. 3:30 Monday afternoon. Are you sure your mom's going to be all right until then? What with Nick home all weekend?"

What? Who the fuck cares, Danny thought. His fingers relaxed now. He had his ride.

"I hope so." He mustered up a concerned look. "Thank you, Beth."

Beth smiled at him, reached over and patted his knee. "It's my pleasure."

Danny felt he had everything covered now. It was just a matter of time before Nick would be in jail and Pam would suffer. Suffer like she made Danny's dad suffer. Danny couldn't wait until he saw his mom on the receiving end of what she did to Jeff. What goes around, comes around, Danny thought. Yeah buddy.

Danny *had* thought of everything. Everything except the one little detail that nobody bothered to mention to him. Nick was on suspension.

While Danny was securing his ride, Jeff was taking care of his own business. That business being his monthly visit to his probation officer. The courthouse wasn't all that far from where he lived so he decided to walk instead of taking a taxi. After all, he thought, the money saved on the cab could be better used to satisfy my urges with Connie the crack-head in the next trailer park over. Jeff wouldn't lower himself to do crack, but he was not above shoving his penis down Connie's throat or between her legs for the low price of ten dollars. So I guess in a way, he mused, we *both* get ten dollars worth of crack.

Jeff reached the parking lot of the courthouse still thinking of his evening plans when he saw a familiar sight. Yes, by this stage in his life the courthouse itself was a familiar sight, but this was something different. He almost missed it, lost in his thoughts. He heard someone laughing and turned his head to see what was going on. His gaze never made it as far as the source of the laughter but right now Jeff didn't care. Just over in the next row of cars, in the area marked Attorneys only, Jeff's gaze stopped. He couldn't believe it. He cut between the row and headed straight towards the white Lincoln towne car parked there. When he got close enough he pulled the stained matchbook out of his wallet and compared the numbers he had written to the car's tag.

"Yes! Yes! Yes!" Jeff jumped up and down, waving

his arms when the numbers matched. He felt like he had
won the lottery.

He noticed people were starting to stare at his
display and regained his composure. All except for his grin,
of course. Jeff looked at the car and matchbook again, and
then at the metal sign above the cars in that row. Parking
for Attorneys only, it said. So, Jeff thought, Mr. Hotshot is
a lawyer. You'd think someone of that caliber could afford
nicer digs than The Mount Vernon Motel and Breakfast
Nook to impress his whores with. Of course, Jeff pondered,
that would be a good indication that Pam isn't the only one
married here. Cheap motel, pay cash, none of those
irritating credit card statements to show up and bite you in
the ass later on.

"Something I can do for you, Sir?" Ted Anders was
sizing up the scruffy looking man standing between him
and his car, grinning like an idiot.

Jeff's grin disappeared. This man is a lot bigger up
close than from the distance I last saw him, he thought as
he took in Ted's full size. He had to think fast. "Uh, maybe
I might be needing a lawyer in the near future so I figured
that since I don't have a phone, this would be the best place
to find one." Jeff pointed at the parking sign. "Is this your
car? Sure is nice."

Ted looked at him skeptically. "Thanks. What
might you need a lawyer for, Mr...?"

163

"Lewis. Hank Lewis. Drunk driving." Jeff figured he better go with what he knows in case this guy asks questions. "You are?" Jeff offered his hand.

"Ted Anders." Drunk driving, I can believe that. Ted thought, looking at the guy's bloodshot eyes and splotchy face. He didn't want to hurt the little guy's feelings but he also had bills to pay and from the looks of this Hank Lewis he figured he'd have to take the case Pro Bono. "I'm sorry Hank. That's not really my field of expertise. You might try the Public Defenders office on the third floor. They do a lot of that sort of thing." Ted smiled and brushed past Jeff to get in his car. "Good luck."

Jeff stood there not the least bit upset by the way he'd just been blown off. Instead, he couldn't believe his luck. Ted Anders. Ted Anders. He kept repeating the name over and over in his head. When Ted drove away Jeff's grin had returned. He walked into the courthouse thinking about what a dumb prick Ted Anders was. His wife must be miserable, what with living with such a self-centered ego like that. In the courthouse restroom Jeff combed his hair and straightened his tee shirt at the mirror. Not my field of expertise, he had told Jeff. No shit. His field of expertise involves whores and sleazy motel rooms, Jeff thought. I bet his wife is a lot nicer. I bet she'd treat me with the respect I deserve. Jeff whistled his way in to see his probation officer feeling very good about things. I bet she'd like to know what I know.

Danny came home from his visit with Beth pleased with himself. He even ate a potted meat sandwich without complaining. Things were back on track again and that's how Danny liked it.

He still couldn't believe he didn't think about it on the night everything happened. That wasn't like him. He always prided himself on being very meticulous in the things he did. They can call it O.C.D. all they want, he thought, but if they're right then how come everything is going according to my plan.

Danny finished his sandwich and tossed the paper plate in the trash. He was pretty sure that his item hadn't been discovered at his mom's. After all, if it had, the shit would have definitely hit the fan by now. Besides, they hadn't even found the vase yet and that's something they know about. Danny was sure Nick and Pam searched his room all over for the vase. Even if they do eventually find that, he thought, it won't bring them any closer. Still, there was always the chance, however slight, that one of them, or even Sally if she goes over there, could stumble across it. I can't take that chance, he thought. I've got to get over there before one of them has a reason to go near the furnace.

With that problem solved and his father out of the house for the time being, Danny felt it was time to test the key. He had waited patiently for the couple of days since he found it for Jeff to go somewhere. He even put the key back in the newspaper later that night when it became apparent that his dad was on his second wind and would be awake for awhile. Danny didn't know how long it would be before he got his chance and he didn't want his father to find out the key was missing in the mean time. It was getting late and he knew his dad would be home soon so he didn't have a lot of time.

Danny went in the bathroom and dug through the cabinet to retrieve his treasure. He found it right where it had always been. Good, he thought. Dad doesn't know I found it. He put the key in his pocket and headed out side for the shed.

Danny didn't know if his dad would be mad if he knew Danny was doing this, but he suspected as much just by the way he hid the key. One thing was for sure, Jeff Nelson didn't want anyone in that shed but Jeff Nelson.

Danny stepped out onto the deck and closed the door behind him. A gentle breeze greeted him as he walked to the shed. When he reached the door he paused for a second trying to figure out what his dad was hiding. He felt a little nervous as he slid the key into the lock and felt it click home.

He gripped the doorknob and took a deep breath. What do I have to be afraid of? He laughed at himself. It's not like my dad keeps the boogy-man in here. Hell,

knowing him it's probably full of beer. He shook his head

and pushed the door open.

CHAPTER VII

Ann Randall was excited. She had received notice that the Roaniks had been assigned their first court date. She would be face to face with that arrogant ass Ted Anders again in less than a week. Thursday, July 17th. The Roaniks file was spread out across her desk and she was going over every detail with a fine tooth comb. The Department's case wasn't looking as good as it did in the beginning. The boy's previous vandalism conviction, if brought up in court could cause the case to go either way. The D.S.S. attorneys weren't going to mention it but Ann was sure that a lawyer of Mr. Anders caliber would. She knew that they would use it as evidence to show that Danny was unstable, that he has a history of delinquent behavior. That could hurt us, she thought. On the other hand, our lawyers will then argue that he was an innocent boy lashing out at the abuse he was receiving at the hands of his stepfather.

While that issue wasn't decisive, Ann thought as

she picked up Justine's report from her visits to the boy and his parents, accompanied with this bullshit it could absolutely destroy our case. Ann glared at the offending pages.

"The mother, Pam Roanik, seems genuinely concerned with her children's well being. The stepfather, Nick Roanik, although in control of anger was resentful of our involvement. He seemed very loyal and protective of the family he married into." Ann couldn't believe what she was reading. She stubbed out her cigarette and turned to the pages covering Justine's visit with Danny and his father.

"Danny Nelson comes across as easily agitated and very manipulative. In talking to him I saw in him a 'one track' way of thinking in that when he would get an idea or want something, that thought alone seemed to override all aspects of rational thinking and logic. Until the particular goal he was focusing on was achieved to his satisfaction, all forms of reasoning with Danny were unsuccessful. Also noted, when Danny would get in this frame of mind, I noticed, his fingers would begin to tap out a pattern of some sort on the table." Ann continued reading the report. How are we supposed to win this thing if our own people are sabotaging us, she thought.

"The father, Jeff Nelson, appeared to me to be cavalier in his role as Danny's guardian and came across as slightly unstable regarding his ex-wife. Although it is early in this investigation, it is this social workers recommendation that Danny be moved to a group home facility where he can be better prepared for the adult world by trained counselors. I also strongly recommend that Danny Nelson be ordered to undergo a psychiatric evaluation concerning what appears to be to this social worker the possibility of Obsessive Compulsive Disorder."

Ann threw the pages down onto the pile on her desk. Why would Justine do this, she thought, she's practically handing Anders a victory in this case. Ann was not about to let that happen. When Ann Randall says a child is abused and neglected, damn it, that child is abused and neglected. She slammed her fist down on the intercom.

"Get me Justine Woodward." She snarled into the microphone.

Several minutes later there was a knock outside her office. "Come in Justine, and close the door." She feigned politeness. When Justine sat down Ann took a breath and regained her composure. "I want to talk to you about your report on the Roanik/Nelson case," she said.

Justine relaxed. "You were right. There's definitely a problem there," she said.

"I know there is, but in reading your report it comes across as if Mr. and Mrs. Roanik are practically Ozzie and Harriet."

"That's because I don't believe that they are the

main problem here. They seemed genuinely concerned about their children's well being."

"Yes, I read that in the report." Ann huffed. "What I didn't see is anything about reasons for them being abusive parents."

"That's because I don't believe they are. Look, they're going to their classes and meetings, they're cooperating, they want help for the boy." Justine paused and rolled her eyes. "That's where I feel the main problem in that family lies. That's what I wrote in my report."

"Let me get this straight." Ann chose her words carefully. "You meet with these people a couple of times, you listen to their sob story, then you visit a hurt boy. Hurt, confused, and his whole world is disrupted so he acts a little agitated. So then you *feel* that he is the main problem? If I didn't know better I'd think this was your first week on the job! He's a teenager, Justine, you know they have enough trouble expressing things under the best circumstances let alone after being smacked around for God knows how long."

"You weren't there, Ann." Justine leaned forward. "This is not your average teenager. No, this is not my first week on the job. I've dealt with my share of teenagers over the many years I've been a social worker and I can honestly say that I've never come across one as cunning as Danny Nelson. Yes, I do feel that he is the main problem. I also agree with the Roaniks, the boy needs some counseling."

"You weren't hired for your feelings, Justine. As a representative of D.S.S. you know as well as I do that our job with these families is to be impartial in our investigations. You dig through the lies on both sides and try to piece together as much of the truth as you can. Now, I want you to re-write this report keeping that in mind and I need it by Monday. We have a court date on Thursday and I have no intention of losing it based on your *feelings*. Remember, our job is to be impartial." She smiled at Justine and held the report out to her.

Justine sat in shock. "Our job is to be impartial, I agree. It is also our job to help the families that need us. Our goal is not to win court cases just because we *feel* that the opposing side made us look like an ass in front of our subordinates. Now, I'll change the part of my report that could show bias, but because this is so important to you I won't make you wait until Monday." Justine snatched the papers from Ann and stood up. She then looked them over and grabbed a pen from Ann's desk and started writing. After only a few seconds she handed the pages back to Ann and said with a huff before walking out, "If that doesn't show impartiality in your eyes, I'll be happy to get the Director of Social Services to show me how to do it better. Good day."

Ann Randall clenched the report and stared after

Justine. Who the hell does she think she is, threatening me? she thought.

After a few minutes Ann calmed down enough to read the revisions. She walked around her desk, sat down and lit a cigarette. She went over the entire report three times before slamming her fist on the desk.

"Son of a bitch!" she yelled. Her eyes fixed on the only revision Justine had made. Justine had crossed out the words 'I feel' on the report and replaced it with 'in my professional opinion'.

Danny pushed the shed door open and peered inside. It was too dark to see anything so he felt along the wall just inside the door for a light switch. When he found it he turned around and looked up and down the street before switching it on and slipping inside.

"Well, I was right about one thing," he said, closing the door behind him. He smiled at the stack of twelve packs standing against the wall beside the door. His smile faded quickly when he turned around to take in the whole shed. "What the hell is going on here?" he said as his mind processed the other items in there.

All three of the walls other than the one with the door were covered with pictures of Pam. Danny looked closely at some of them. Not all of them were of his mother alone. Some were of her and Jeff. Danny started looking

173

from the wall on his left and noticed a sort of progression in the pattern of photos. In the first ones Jeff and Pam looked young. If not his age then not much older. At the corner connecting the wall to his left to the wall opposite were a group of pictures of Pam and Jeff's wedding. That second wall contained photos from throughout their marriage. Danny remembered some of them. He looked over the whole wall as he went through a roller coaster of emotions. They looked so happy, he thought.

While looking through the pictures of his parents' marriage one thing became painfully clear to Danny. There was not one picture of Sally or him. The closest he could find in the whole assortment was a picture of a very pregnant Pam. Everything else was either just Pam or Pam and Jeff.

When Danny got to the third wall he jumped back in horror. The first picture was the photo of his mom and Nick with their wedding announcement from the newspaper. Directly under his mom's smiling face someone had written in red marker the word whore. Danny looked over the other pictures on that wall. There were fewer pictures on the third wall than on the previous two but they were all more recent. They all also had one thing in common other than the subject. Under every picture of Pam, in red marker was the word whore.

Most of the pictures on the third wall were

newspaper cut-outs. A few, like the one of his mom's house, were from a camera. The caption under that one, Danny noticed, read 'home sweet whore'. Danny tried to remember when his dad took that picture. He couldn't ever remember Jeff owning a camera.

There were also newspaper pictures from when his dad was arrested, including a blown up version of Jeff's mug shot tacked up there.

While Danny tried to figure out what all this meant, he got even more confused when he finally noticed the other things in the shed. There was a cot on one side of the room that was fully made up. Sheets and all. Lying on top of it, in all its glory was a fully inflated blow-up doll with an 8x10 picture of Danny's mother taped over its face and the word whore written in red across its breasts. In and around the trash can beside the cot were wads of crumpled up tissue.

Danny began to feel nauseous while he tried to find some kind of explanation for what he was seeing. He could find none. He suddenly wished he had never found the key. Danny didn't want to see anymore. He closed his eyes and backed up towards the door. A million thoughts were racing through his head at once and none of them made sense.

He felt the door behind him and turned around to open it. He desperately wanted out of there. Not even thinking or caring if someone saw him, he turned off the light and left the shed as quick as he could. His hands were shaking so bad that it took three tries before he could get the key in the slot to lock it back up.

When he regained himself he put the key back in the newspaper in the bathroom and splashed cold water on his face. Danny stood there at the sink looking at his reflection in the mirror for a few minutes thinking. He didn't know what to make of what he saw in the shed but he did know one thing. There was no way he could tell Beth or anybody else about it.

Pam was glad that her husband had some errands to do on Saturday. She desperately needed to talk to Ted. She had screwed up, she knew that. She never should have slept with Nick's best friend. What the hell had she been thinking?

Pam called Ted that morning after Nick had left and told him she needed to meet with him. When he suggested they meet at a motel Pam told him no, could they meet at his office. On the way there she began to worry about how Ted would take what she had to tell him. Oh, he'll understand. She tried to convince herself. It was just a one time thing. He has to know that. I was vulnerable. Everything in my life was falling apart and Nick was so wrapped up in his own feelings about everything that was happening to us. He wasn't there when I needed him. Ted was there, comforting me and it got out of hand. He knows that's all it was. Or does he, she thought. If that's the case then how come he wanted to meet me at a motel?

Pam pulled her car into the lot beside Ted's office building. Since it was Saturday, the only other car in the lot was Ted's. It's no big deal, Pam thought as she looked around the area before exiting her car. Just a lawyer and his client meeting to go over their upcoming case. To be safe though, or maybe out of shame, Pam put on her sunglasses and walked quickly with her head down until she got into the lobby of the building. She took the elevator to the third floor, taking slow, deep breaths until the door opened and she saw him standing in the corridor outside of his office.

When Ted heard the elevator door open he turned around and saw Pam. "Don't worry, baby, we're all alone here. Except for the janitor, but he's already finished this floor. Come on. Let's get you out of that cold elevator and into something warm, like my arms." Ted held his hand out to her.

Before Pam could react, his hand was around hers and he was pulling her toward him. Ted led her into his office and shut the door behind them.

Ted turned and wrapped his arms around Pam's waist and said, "I have to admit it surprised me when you said you wanted to meet here. This will be a first for me, too." He smiled and leaned in to kiss her. There lips almost touched before Pam, who hadn't said so much as hello up till then, turned her head. She had come there for a reason and this was not it. No matter how it felt, she was determined not to give in. She loved Nick.

"Ted, wait," she said, ducking out of his arms. "I came here to talk to you." Pam smiled weakly and walked past the leather couch, opting instead for the chair opposite the desk. She wanted to keep some distance between the two of them.

Ted Anders nodded, smoothed out his shirt and sat down on the corner of his desk directly in front of her. "All right, Doll, what's on your mind?" he asked, sensing something.

Pam took a breath. "I want to talk to you about the other day," her gaze went to the floor, "at the motel."

Ted lifted her chin up and caught her eye. "It was great, wasn't it?"

She pulled back and shook her head. "No. I mean yes. What I mean is that what happened between us, I felt was special. I needed the closeness, to feel needed. I was dealing with so much and I, you were there."

Ted didn't like where this was going. He stood up and walked around behind his desk and sat in his chair. "Let me guess. This is the part where you say that you were vulnerable. That I took advantage of you in your hour of need. Is that it? Because if that's what you…"

"No, Ted," she pleaded, "Yes, I was vulnerable, but I take my share of the blame for what we did. I just think we should forget it ever happened. No one gets hurt. A mistake that no one has to know about."

Ted thought for a moment, drumming his fingers on his desk as he glared at her. The seconds dragged on and Pam began to see just how big of a mistake it really had been.

"Ted?" she asked, nervously. "Don't you think that's the best way to handle this?"

"You fucking tease," he mumbled.

Pam looked at him in horror. "What?"

"You fucking cock tease!" Ted slammed his fist on the desk. When he did Pam jumped. "You make love to me all afternoon and then get a sudden attack of guilt, so I'm supposed to forget it happened so you can live with yourself? Is that it? Is it?"

Pam looked towards the door, wishing she could crawl under it. This was not the Ted Anders she knew. She thought he would understand. What was he doing? "Ted, wait," she begged, "I'm sorry it happened. It was stupid. Think about Nora, and Nick. He's your best friend. You don't want to hurt them."

"Think about Nora and Nick? That's a laugh. Were you thinking about them when you had your mouth around my dick? What was it for you anyway? Payment for services rendered? You watch my kid and I'll sleep with you? Was that it? If anything, you seduced me," Ted seethed.

Pam started shaking. "What are you saying? I thought you'd understand. I thought you were our friend?"

Ted leaned back in his chair and smiled. "Oh, I do understand. I understand that you use your body to get what you want. And yes, I am your friend, Nick's too. I'd feel just awful if he were to learn that his loving wife seduced his friend while he's got the possibility of not only career ruin, but jail time hanging over his head. Knowing Nick, and I do, I believe that would kill him. And poor Nora, why, she would definitely leave me if she found out I wasn't a strong enough man to resist your advances. Of course if that were to happen, then that whole temporary custody agreement regarding Sally would become null and void. Poor Sally, I'd hate to see her subjected to foster care, or worse. Then again, D.S.S. might see fit to send her to live with her father and Danny. They do like to keep siblings together if possible. Yes Pam, I would hate to see any of that happen." Ted stood up and walked around to Pam's chair and looked at her directly. "Luckily we *are* friends, so I'm sure we can find a way to work together to make sure none of it does happen." He then winked at her and walked over to sit on the couch.

Pam sat in her chair stunned. Did I just hear what I think I heard? She was aghast. Am I being blackmailed by this creature? This can not be happening. She turned to look at him, sitting on the end of the couch, patting the space next to him. Her fear turned to rage as she saw the smug look on his face. Only it wasn't Ted Anders face she saw in that office. It was her father's. She turned her face away in disgust. Her hands trembled as her anger grew.

"I will not be a victim to you or anyone else ever again, Daddy!" she said slowly between clenched teeth.

"Daddy." Ted smiled. "Now you're getting into the spirit of things. Come over here, Baby, and call me daddy. I'll make you forget all…"

Before he could finish his sentence Pam flew out of her chair and, grabbing the letter opener from Ted's desk, jumped on top of him slamming her knee into his groin.

"Aauugghh!" He screamed as the weight of her body landed directly on his manhood.

"Let me tell you something, *Daddy,* and I don't mean that in a good way," Pam said as she simultaneously ground her knee farther into his crotch and dug the tip of the letter opener against the side of his neck, "You are going to defend Nick to the utmost of your ability as a lawyer. You are going to push the judge to give us back custody of my daughter, and you are never going to speak of what happened between us to anyone. You are going to do all of this willingly and without, let me be clear on this, without ever again sticking your pathetic little penis anywhere in or around my body." Pam ground her knee again and twisted the opener a little deeper to make sure she was getting her point across. She saw by the tears in his eyes and his not so pleasurable moaning that she was.

"Let me explain something to you, lover boy. My husband and kids are my life. If I lose them I've got nothing. If I've got nothing," she dug deeper and paused to look at the trickle of blood that was now sliding down his neck, "you've got nothing. Now, as friends, do we understand each other?"

Ted tried to speak but couldn't. He nodded instead.

Pam didn't move for a moment and looked into his eyes to see if he was lying. His eyes pleaded that he was telling the truth. She then pulled the letter opener away from his neck and slowly stood up, never taking her eyes off of him. Her breathing was fast and her heart raced but she never felt so free in her life.

"You better be more careful shaving, that's a nasty cut you gave yourself." Pam tossed the box of tissues from the desk to the spot on the couch Ted had been patting just moments before.

Ted however, was too busy cradling his swollen testicles through his pants to notice. After a few minutes he was able to get his breath and speak.

"You've got spunk. I like that." He whimpered, trying unsuccessfully to regain his dignity. "You present a good argument. We'll handle it your way. I think," he looked up and saw the glare of determination on her face and the letter opener still in her hand. "I mean I hope we're done here. Would you mind showing yourself out?" He grunted as he fell over onto his side and curled up in the fetal position, his hands still massaging his balls.

Pam looked at him and almost laughed. In a matter of minutes Ted had gone from big man blackmailer to crying like a baby, and all because of her. She wished she had had the courage to do that years ago with her father. Hell, she thought, I wouldn't have even needed the letter opener with him. One quick bite and that asshole never would have touched another little girl again.

"I can see that we're done here. It was good seeing you, Ted. Feel free to lay there and get your rest, you'll need to be in top form to get our case ready." She smiled sweetly at him and tossed the letter opener on to the desk. "Oh and why don't you give Nick a call, he's going through so much right now and he could use a friend."

Ted just groaned as Pam walked out into the corridor. He could hear her whistling as she waited for the elevator. He moaned even louder when he recognized the song just before he passed out. Jerry Lee Lewis, *Great Balls of Fire*

What Goes Around   by Mick Woodhall

CHAPTER VIII

Nick had finished his errands a couple hours before Pam got home. When she walked in the door after her meeting with Ted she found her husband sitting on the couch with a sad look on his face. That asshole Ted double crossed me was her first thought. She closed the door behind her and went over to sit by Nick.

"Honey?" she began cautiously. "What's wrong? You look upset." Pam put her hand on his shoulder.

"Hi, Baby, oh I guess it's all hitting home now. That this is real and not just some bad joke." He sighed.

Pam was confused. "What do you mean? Did something happen?"

Nick picked up a letter from the coffee table and handed it to his wife. "This came in the mail today."

Pam took the letter and when she unfolded it she let out a sigh of relief. It was from the Clerk of the Court. Ted hadn't screwed her over, not yet anyway. "They've given us a court date? Is that what's troubling you? Nick, Honey, this is good news. It says here that we have to appear on Thursday. This could all be over in less than a week." She looked at him.

Nick stood up and began to pace. "It could be over, yes, or it could just be the start of the next level of even more shit." He stopped directly in front of her and looked down into her eyes. "Right now I'm on suspension. Not just from my job but in my, or should I say our, whole lives." He shook his head and raised his hands up as if to gesture, what next. "I could go to jail. Hell, even if I'm found guilty and just get probation my career is ruined. And what about us? Can our marriage stand a jail sentence? Then there's Sally. What happens to her?"

Nick was talking a mile a minute now. Pam sat patiently listening while he got it out of his system. She did notice that throughout his list of worries, Danny wasn't mentioned. She understood, but Danny was still her son so that hurt her.

"Honey, it'll all work out." She stood and pulled Nick into her arms, looking lovingly into his eyes. "I have faith in Ted. I bet he'll work harder on our case than any other one he's had. If for no other reason than because you're his best friend. D.S.S. doesn't have a case. You were at work when all that happened, remember? They're grasping at straws and Ted will prove it. Besides," she nuzzled his ear and whispered, "even if it does go sour, we always have conjugal visits to look forward to."

Nick slapped her lightly on her ass and told her that wasn't helping matters.

"Careful Honey, that's domestic violence you know," she teased.

Nick pulled away. "I know you're trying to cheer me up, but I'm really worried about what can happen. Look at the damage it's all ready done to Sally."

Pam saw that he was serious. The two of them had always used humor as a tool to deal with rough times, but this was the toughest they had ever faced and in Nick's case it was no longer a joking matter.

"Nick, look at me." Pam cupped his face in her hands so he couldn't turn away. "We will get through this. We're strong, and Sally's strong. She'll bounce back from it and so will we. Trust me." She kissed her husbands forehead and smiled.

Nick started to feel better. "Well, either way at least we'll know something." He sighed. "I suppose that's better than this limbo we've been living in all this time. You're right, Ted will do his best. That's what friends do for each other. I'd better call him. Let him know we have a court date." Nick reached for the phone.

Pam stopped him. "Why don't you wait, Honey, it's the weekend. Besides, they would have sent him the same notice that we got, wouldn't they? Let's go grab some dinner, set this aside and have a nice evening out. You can call him Monday morning. First thing."

Pam was relieved when Nick reluctantly agreed

with her and set the phone back in its cradle. She had left Ted in pretty bad shape and she wanted to be sure that he had sufficient time to deal with his bruised ego before Nick talked to him. After all, a man in pain might say the wrong thing.

On Monday morning Danny pretended to be asleep until his father left for the day. Jeff was going to make a few bucks helping some guy lay out a gravel driveway. That was just fine with Danny. He hadn't been able to look his father in the eye all weekend.

Danny was still very disturbed and bewildered by what he saw in the shed. The stuff in there, he thought, could not be from my dad. It must be a joke. Maybe someone's playing a trick on him. My dad is a decent man who's just a little down on his luck. He's not some sick twisted pervert. Danny's head was starting to hurt trying to figure it all out.

"I can't let this distract me." He mumbled as he climbed off the couch that had been his bed since he came to live there. "Today is the day. Timing is everything. He called over to his mom's house and hung up when the answering machine picked up. "Perfect. No one's home."

By the time he showered and got dressed it was close to 1:00. He tried the number again and still was greeted by the answering machine. Smiling, he laid the phone back down without leaving a message. "It's almost time," he said aloud, looking at his watch. "I better go and make sure Beth remembered, and is ready."

Danny walked the short distance to Beth's trailer and knocked on the door.

When Beth opened it she saw Danny and was surprised. "Hi Danny. You're a little early, aren't you?" she said while looking at her watch.

Danny was always early. It was the one obsession that he would admit to. Just the thought of being late for something, anything, would make his palms sweat. "Yeah, I guess so. I hope you don't mind, I got kind of bored waiting around," he lied.

"Well, I've got a few things to do before I take you over to your mom's, but you can come along if you'd like," she said.

"If you're sure you don't mind. I have to be at her house at 3:30 though. That's when she's expecting me."

"Oh, you talked to her? How's she doing?" Beth's face lit up.

Shit, thought Danny. Why'd she go and ask that? "She sounded okay, but she said she couldn't talk. I think Nick was there. We'll be alone today if we get there at 3:30."

"Well, let's see what we can do." She grabbed her purse and keys and led Danny out the door. "Hop in," she said when they reached her car.

The things she had to take care of consisted of a quick oil change, a stop at Wal-Mart, and getting her hair cut. This last stop was bringing them very close to 3:30. Danny went outside while Beth sat in the salon chair giggling with the portly woman who was trimming her split ends. Danny didn't give a rat's ass about her split ends. He needed to get going. He sat on a bench in front of the salon and quietly tapped on the armrest. Each passing minute brought them closer to failure and he could not have that. Not now. He looked over his shoulder and saw the two women just chatting away like they had all day to cut her hair. Danny looked at his watch. 3:15. "Damn!" he said so loud an elderly couple walking by turned to look at him. He glared right back at them. "Do they have to cut it one strand at a time?" he snarled. The couple turned and hurried along.

"Do you know them?" Beth's voice was behind him.

"What? No." He studied her face to see if she had heard his outburst. Feeling sure she hadn't, he continued. "Just saying hello. You know, being polite to your elders, that sort of thing." Danny smiled. "Your hair looks good. Are you ready?" he asked hoping there were no more stops.

"Thank you, and yes. I'm ready to meet your mother." She smiled back at him.

Danny stopped short when she said this. He knew

he better think quick. They got in the car and she started driving in the direction Danny told her.

"Do me a favor." Danny chose his words carefully. "When we get there, would you mind waiting in the car while I go in?" He looked at her for a response and saw it all over her face. Hurt. "What I mean is…"

"You asked me to drive you over to see your mother and now you want me to sit in the car like some cab driver?"

Danny stared as a lone tear made its way down her cheek. "No, it's not like that. Please listen," he pleaded. He was too close now to have her get pissed off and take him back to his dad's trailer. "What I meant was that I don't know what I'll be walking into. My mom is a very private person. For all I know he could have beat the shit out of her last night and she's all covered in bruises. Then here I come with a complete stranger and she'll be all embarrassed and stuff." He paused. "Just please wait in the car until I can talk to her for a few minutes, then if she's up to it I'd be proud to introduce you."

Beth sniffled and nodded her head. "I guess I can understand that. I wouldn't want a bunch of strangers in my home if I had just been beaten up. I hope she's okay though. I would like to meet her."

Danny sat back in his seat, relieved. "I hope so, too," he lied. "I'm sure she'd love to meet you as well.

Hopefully she'll be up for it."

The rest of the ride went with out a hitch with Danny giving directions and Beth singing along with the radio. Danny enjoyed her voice and told her so. She smiled and thanked him as he pointed to the driveway.

"This is where you used to live?" She whistled. "They must do all right. This is nice."

Yeah, yeah, yeah, they did all right taking everything from my dad to buy this place. Danny fumed. "I'll come out in a minute and let you know if it's OK for you to come in." Danny got out of the car without waiting for a response and began digging in his pocket for his key.

When he reached the porch he looked up and down the street before unlocking the door and slipping inside. Good, no sign of Nick or Pam, he thought, closing the door behind him.

Nick was running out of things to do to occupy his time. He had talked to Ted that morning and yes, Ted did know about the court date. Ted also assured his friend that he was making their case his top priority and that would he tell Pam that as well. After that call Nick felt better about things. It wasn't that he had doubted Ted's dedication. No, he had been more concerned about the possibility of going to jail. He felt that there was no more qualified lawyer than Ted Anders to make sure that didn't happen but as anyone

192

who had ever had the possibility of prison time dangling over their head can attest, even the best lawyer or nicest Judge were not a 100% guarantee of you walking out of there a free man.

Court was only a few days away and Nick desperately needed a distraction, something to occupy his mind. Work would have been a good outlet but when he called Ernie, his boss still stood firm. Call me after the hearing, he had told Nick. What a laugh. Nick knew damn well that a Channel 11 news crew would be at the court house on Thursday. He also knew Channels 9 and 5 would be there as well. A bunch of vultures, he thought, ready and eager to hang one of their own.

Nick decided to clear his mind by doing some work around the house. Pam had been on him about the sink leaking in the kitchen for what seemed to him like forever so he figured he'd start there.

He stopped by the hardware store to get some plumbing supplies before meeting up with Pam for lunch. While they ate he told her about his conversation with Ted. She seemed genuinely relieved that Ted was working so hard on their case. If Nick hadn't been so mentally distracted he might have noticed how odd she acted when he told her, but he didn't.

She was also pleased that he was finally getting around to fixing the sink. It'll do you good, she told him.

Stay productive and stop worrying. Words of wisdom, he thought.

They finished their lunch and Nick dropped her off back at work.

"Are you going home to start on the sink now, Honey?" she asked.

"I've got one more stop to make and then I'm on it." Nick answered. "I'll see you this evening, okay. I love you." He leaned over to her side of the car and kissed her.

"I love you, too." She purred when they pulled apart. Pam got out and blew Nick another kiss before turning and going into her office building.

Danny didn't bother to turn on the lights. He saw no point in it. He knew where he had to go. Where he had to look. First he needed to check something. He went down the hall to what used to be his bedroom and opened the door. A familiar feeling overcame him when he entered the room. All of his stuff was still where he left it. Did they even come in here to look for it, he thought. He went over and sat down on his bed. Bouncing up and down on it he had to admit to himself that he did miss a soft bed to sleep in. It was much better than that old lumpy couch at his dad's place.

Before he got too nostalgic he remembered he was limited on time and still had something to do. He opened his closet door and right away knew something was different. Shit, he thought. They have been in here. He looked the closet over and noticed the box that Nick had rearranged. "Damn!" he growled. "Couldn't they have at least put things back the way they're supposed to go? I don't have time to straighten out this mess."

With one hand fiercely tapping on the door jamb, the other reached towards the box. Get a hold of yourself! A voice in his head screamed at him. If you fix it back, they'll know you were here. Stay focused. You can fix it when this is all over. Get on with it!

Danny knew the voice was right. Knowing it and doing it are two different things though. He stood there for several minutes with his hand on the box. The only sound in the room was the sound of a certain rhythm gradually going from a soft tapping to a loud pounding on the closet door jamb. It wasn't until Danny's fingers started to cramp up that he was able to get a hold of himself again. He took a few deep breaths and let go of the box to massage his fingers.

When the cramp finally faded Danny looked down at the closet floor. At least that didn't look like it's been messed with. He told himself. Squatting down on one knee he pried the floorboard loose. He reached in and pulled out the vase. When he saw the dried blood on the side of it his hand went to his nose, long since healed. Sometimes you've got to make sacrifices for the cause; he remembered thinking on that night, just before he smacked the vase against his face. As he studied the vase he thought how long ago it had happened, and just how much it had hurt.

"Well," he said aloud, "at least that mystery is solved, Scooby." Knowing for certain that they hadn't found the vase put Danny at ease. He gently put it back in the hole and slid the floorboard over it, making sure it was intact. "One more thing to do." He said as he stood up. Danny took one last look at the box on the shelf and then headed towards the basement.

Beth was getting tired of sitting in the Roaniks driveway. Hasn't Danny had enough time to find out if his mother wants to meet me or not, she wondered. She looked at her watch. I'll give him five more minutes and then I'm going in there anyway. Besides, I've got to go to the bathroom.

Lost in her thoughts, Beth didn't notice the SUV that had slowly rolled up beside her and parked.

"Can I help you, miss?" came a voice off to her left.

Beth turned to see a nice looking man holding a bag from a hardware store in one hand and a bouquet of roses in the other.

Nick asked the question again. "Are you all right? How can I help you?"

Beth knew who he was. She was speechless at first.

196

Wasn't he supposed to be at work, preparing the news?

That's what Danny had told her. Then she understood. She

looked at the flowers he was holding then looked at the

front door. That's why Danny hasn't come out yet, she

thought. The bastard did beat her up, and now he comes

waltzing home with a bunch of lousy roses and probably

some fake apology full of empty promises of how it will

never happen again. That sorry piece of shit. How typical.

    The more Beth thought about it the madder she got.

That poor woman in there, what can I…?

    Her thoughts were cut off as Nick approached her

car and leaned over. "Cat got your tongue? Are you looking

for someone?" he asked smiling.

    Beth cringed when he leaned closer. "You stay

away from me, you bastard!" she hissed at Nick. "You may

get away with that shit on her, but if you touch me I'll

scream and Danny will call the police!" She pointed at the

house.

    Nick straightened back up as if he'd been sucker

punched. First he comes home to this crazy woman in his

driveway, babbling some kind of nonsense. Then she

threatens him with Danny. What the hell is going on? He

thought. "Danny?"

    "Damn right, tough guy! He's right inside and

believe me…"

    Nick didn't wait to hear any more. He sprinted to

the front door. What the hell is Danny doing here? He wondered. He flung the door open and ran inside. Nick ran from room to room looking for him and was becoming even more bewildered at the whole situation when he couldn't find him.

Then he heard a noise coming from the basement. Nick bounded for the stairs and leapt down them three at a time. When he hit the landing he turned the corner and saw Danny walking past the laundry room in the direction of the furnace.

"Just what in the hell do you think you're doing here?" Nick demanded.

Danny froze in his tracks. His heart jumped and his breathing stopped as he slowly turned around. "Oh. Hi Nick. How have you been?" He said in as calm of a voice as he was able to muster. Danny was screwed and he knew it. "Nice flowers. Sorry I didn't get you anything."

Nick was dumbfounded. He turned his eyes from Danny to the roses he was still holding. Hi Nick? This kid breaks into my house and has the nerve to ask me how I've been? "I'll tell you how I've been."

Nick's stare was now as cold as stone and it was drilling so deep into Danny's head that Danny could feel it. He had never seen Nick look this way. For the first time that he could remember, he was frightened.

"I'm about to do to you what I've already been

198

accused of if you don't give me a damn good reason for being here." Nick told him. In the time it took him to say it Nick had closed the distance between them to three short feet, his eyes never wavering.

"I wanted to see mom. I miss her. I was able to get a ride over and was hoping she was here, that's all." Danny stammered.

"That's all, all right. All bullshit!" Nick had backed the boy against his work bench at this point and it was taking everything he had not to knock Danny on his ass. "If that's true, which we both know it's not, then what are you doing in the basement? You knew she wasn't home when you came in the door. Hell, knowing you, you knew she wasn't here before you even came over. Isn't that true?" Nick, towering over him, was in his face now. He could see the fear in Danny's eyes. "Last chance kid. Tell the truth for once, if you can remember how."

Danny's eyes shifted for a second and in that time Nick saw the fear wash away and was replaced with a look of triumph. "Please don't hit me, Nick!" Danny begged with a grin that Nick could see, but was blocked from Beth's view by the angle in which she stood since coming down a moment before. "I just want to see my mom!" Danny continued.

Nick studied Danny's sudden change and before he could decide if it was a bluff, he knew it wasn't.

"Don't you lay a hand on him, you bastard!" Beth screamed from behind Nick, causing him to spin around in surprise. That gave Danny the opportunity to move away from him and run over to stand in front of Beth; protectively shielding her while he faced Nick.

"Let's get out of here. He won't do anything with a witness around. He never does," Danny said, while staring at a fuming Nick. He gently nudged Beth to the stairs and she started up. Just before following her Danny turned back to Nick, giving him a grin even bigger than his dad's famous one and said, "You really need to learn to control your anger, Nick. Perhaps you should look into anger management classes. I understand D.S.S. offers a good one."

Before Nick could recover from what just went on, Danny and Beth were out the door. He picked up the flowers and plumbing supplies that he had dropped and started to go upstairs to call a locksmith. That kid is more unstable and conniving than we ever imagined, he thought after he ordered all the locks in the house changed. "I hate to say it," he said aloud to no one while reaching for a beer, "but that kid is dangerous."

"Are you all right? Did he hurt you?" Beth asked Danny after they got back on the main road.

"I'm fine," Danny grumbled. What the hell was Nick doing home anyway, he asked himself. If I had had just five more minutes I could have gotten what I needed and been out of there. Fuck that bastard. How am I going to get in there again? My key is useless now. No doubt he started changing the locks the minute he quit wetting himself. Danny smiled at the thought of the look on Nick's stupid face when Beth came down. It was priceless.

"Danny? Do you think we should go to the police and report what he did?" Beth asked.

Danny turned to look at her. Was she serious? We can't report that. I wasn't even allowed to be in there. How can a girl be both this pretty and this stupid at the same time? Still, she didn't know I wasn't allowed there, he reasoned. Besides, she probably saved me from a severe beating. One that Nick would have gotten away with too. Danny thought hard. I know I can turn this whole thing to my advantage and hopefully get what I went there for, too.

"No Beth," he finally answered, "He might take that out on my mom. She's been through so much as it is. I don't want to be the cause of her misery."

"You are just the sweetest, most caring guy I've ever met." At the stop sign she leaned over and kissed his cheek.

When she did, Danny felt flushed and the heat raced to his groin, which awakened like a bear out of hibernation. He didn't have time to enjoy the feeling because it stopped as quickly as it started when Beth spoke again.

"By the way, where was your mom? I thought she was going to meet you there. I didn't see her."

Damn she asks a lot of questions. "I don't know." He said innocently. "I looked all over the house before that asshole chased me into the basement. Maybe she found out he was coming home early and didn't want to be there."

"Wouldn't she have called and let you know."

"I'm sure she tried. Remember we left a couple of hours early though so she couldn't have reached me. My dad doesn't have an answering machine so I guess I'll have to ask her when I talk to her next." Danny hoped this put an end to the inquisition. Thankfully it did. They rode the rest of the way in silence.

Pam pulled into her driveway just as the locksmiths were leaving. When she came in the house she found Nick sitting at the kitchen table pouring over a stack of pamphlets from different alarm companies.

"Nick?" she asked suspiciously. "Looking into some home improvements are you? I was just hoping for the faucet to stop dripping."

Nick just sat there, studying alarm features. Oblivious that she had even come in. She watched him a moment then dropped her purse on top of the article he was reading.

"Hi, Honey I'm home!" she bellowed.

Nick looked up at his wife. "We've had company."

"Oh my God!" Pam fell into the chair beside him. "The locksmith, these alarm brochures, was the house broken into? Were you here? Are you hurt? Let me look at you. Is anything missing?" She studied Nick's face.

"I don't think anything's missing. And yes, I was here. Well, not when it happened, but luckily I arrived before he left."

"He? Did you get a good look at him?"

"I can do better than that. I can tell you his name."

Pam looked in her husbands eyes. Something strange was going on here. Where were the police? "Okay, Honey, give me his name."

Nick took her hand. "I can't. You all ready gave it to him."

"Damn it Nick, quit screwing around. Who broke into our home and why didn't you call the police?"

"Danny did, and to answer your second question, because I love you."

"What! My Danny? Our Danny? What for?" Pam didn't know what to think. "Is he all right? Where is he now?"

"That depends on what you mean by all right. Physically he seemed fine. He's lost some weight though. Mentally, well that's a different story all together." Nick hid the disgust he felt when his wife said *our* Danny.

203

"What does that mean?"

Nick told her the whole story. Even admitting that he wanted to deck her son. Not admitting how badly though.

Pam sat for a moment in astonishment when he finally finished. When she collected her thoughts she began by telling him she understood why he wanted to hit Danny, but thanking him for not doing it. She also kissed him and thanked him for not calling the police.

"Well to be totally honest, with that girl as a witness and with what I'm already charged with, throw that on top of Danny's acting abilities, if I had called the cops you could very well have come home to find both your son and husband in jail.

"Yes, I guess you're right. Who was the girl? Have you ever seen her before?"

"No, but I got a good look at the car and I'd be willing to bet it can be found in front of one of the trailers in Jeff's park."

"What do you think he was after?"

"I don't know. At first I thought it might be that vase, but when I found him he was in the basement. If I remember right he never went to the basement that night, did he?"

"No, he went straight to his room until the police arrived. Do you think maybe he moved it from where it was to a better hiding place down there, Nick?"

"It's possible, I guess, but when he went to retrieve it from where ever he had it and saw that it hadn't been found wouldn't you think he'd feel safer just leaving it there?"

"You'd think that, but like you said, he's not rational."

"That's why I've been looking at these." Nick told her while pointing at the alarm company brochures.

"Do you really think we need to go to that extreme? He is only a boy."

"A very manipulating, dangerous boy, Pam."

"Dangerous? How can he be dangerous?"

"You didn't see him, Pam, his eyes. There was no remorse in them. No guilt. He planned this whole thing, right from the beginning. Don't you see that now? He's got a goal. There is something in this house, most likely in the basement that he needs either to achieve that goal or, if someone else gets a hold of it, can prevent him from achieving it. It's up to us to figure out his agenda, before court if possible."

"Nick. Aren't you over imagining things just a little? He probably started this whole thing just to get attention, either from his father or us. Then it got out of hand and blew up in his face. How can one teenager orchestrate something so massive that it involves his family, D.S.S., and the courts? He's just a kid who needs help. He's not the puppet master."

Nick sighed and turned back to his pamphlets. He was slowly realizing that there was no way he could think of to make his wife understand that her precious son was more disturbed than either of them had previously suspected. He felt that she knew it, but getting her to accept and admit it would take time. Time that Nick didn't feel they had. If Danny would go so far as breaking and entering on top of everything else, Nick wondered, how much farther he would go to get whatever it is that he's after? It was then that Nick decided that maybe it was time to bring in a professional. An unknown face that could sort of keep tabs on Danny and let Nick know what he's up to. I guess we'll finally find out just how good you are at what you do, Charlie Tibbens, Nick thought.

With that, Nick put away the alarm brochures, smiled at his wife and gave her the flowers that he had left lying on the counter beside the refrigerator.

The next morning, after Pam left for work, Nick looked up Charlie's number in the yellow pages under Private Investigator. Charlie Tibbens answered on the third ring.

CHAPTER IX

"Tibbens investigations, how can we help you?" came the voice through the line.

"Charlie? We need to talk."

"We are talking. Now tell me who you are so I know who I'm talking to."

"Sorry. This is Nick. Nick Roanik. We met in..." Nick didn't get to finish.

"Jail. We met in jail. How's things going pal?" Charlie laughed. "I had a feeling I'd be hearing from you."

"Yeah, well, that's one for you. I never thought I'd need you, but can I come by your office. As I said, we need to talk." Nick hoped he wasn't too busy to meet with him right away.

"Sure, pal." Charlie said. "Is everything all right?"

"I hope so." Nick sighed. All of this was wearing on him. "I just need to hire you to do what you do best."

"What? Piss people off?" Charlie laughed again.

"Why would I want to pay you for that? You seem

to like doing that Pro Bono." Nick was not in the mood for bullshit. He needed a professional, not a smart ass. When he told Charlie this, Charlie apologized and told him to come right over.

When Charlie gave Nick the address he was surprised. Not only was his office located in a very upscale building downtown, it was also the same building that Ted Anders practiced law in.

"This is really nice, Charlie." Nick said when he arrived. "It's not at all what I expected."

"Still judging books by their covers, huh?" Charlie shook Nick's hand and pointed to a chair. "I told you before. This job isn't like what you see in the movies. We don't all work out of dank, run down offices and drink ourselves to sleep every night. You said you wanted a professional. Now how professional would you think me if I asked you to meet me in some run down dive bar in the middle of the afternoon?"

"As I recall," Nick took a seat, "we did meet in a run down dive bar in the middle of the afternoon last time. And I didn't have any pre-conceived TV land ideas of you using an old crack house for an office. What I meant was that judging from the way you dress and that graying mullet you call a hairstyle, that there would be everything from autographed pictures of Rick Springfield on these walls to a model of the General Lee on your desk."

Charlie smiled as he sat down. "Are you saying that my look is a little dated, Nick?"

"Let's just say that as long as you don't change your phone number to 867-5309 I can live with it."

"It's a deal. Now, all kidding aside, what can I do to help?"

Nick leaned forward and told Charlie everything that had happened regarding Danny's break in. Including his feelings on Danny having an agenda as well as what he thought about Danny's mental stability. Charlie sat back in his chair with his chin resting on his finger tips as Nick talked. When Nick was finished, Charlie laced his hands behind his head and let out a whistle.

"Whoa!" he said to Nick. "You've certainly got a live one on your hands! Let me think this through. First, you were right about not calling the police. You're in enough trouble already and if this kid is half as cunning as you say, he probably would have said you kidnapped him. That said, what do you think this agenda, as you call it, of his is? Why is he going through all this trouble to screw you?"

Nick looked at him thoughtfully. "I haven't figured that out yet, but I bet whatever he was doing in my basement is the key."

"Do you think he was looking for something, or hiding something?" Charlie offered.

"I couldn't tell. When I saw him he was walking away from the stairs, toward the back of the basement."

Charlie nodded. "Well, that tells me one thing. Whatever he was trying to do, he hadn't done it yet. You obviously interrupted him before hand."

Nick looked at him, puzzled. "Maybe my reporter skills are dwindling during my suspension Charlie, but I don't get you."

Charlie stood up and walked around the side of his desk. "Think about it. He was heading away from the stairs, not towards them. That says that he wasn't ready to leave, he still had something to do. As far as was he hiding something or looking for something, I believe he was looking for something. You said that when you confronted him his hands were empty. Walking away from the exit with nothing in his hands indicates that he was looking for something and you got there before he could find it. Of course there is the possibility that he wanted to hide something small and it was still in his pocket when you came down, but I doubt that."

Nick was amazed. "Why do you doubt that?"

Charlie smiled. "That's where experience comes in, Pal. If you were doing something that you knew you shouldn't in a place where you shouldn't be and didn't want to get caught, wouldn't you have everything as ready as possible ahead of time?"

"Yes, I guess I would." Nick answered.

"So would most people. I don't care if he snuck in there to hide something as small as a paper clip, he would have had it out of his pocket and in his hand at the ready long before he even got to the basement. Even the most inexperienced burglars know that time is of the essence and aren't going to risk getting caught by wasting precious time digging in their pocket for something they could have all ready had out."

Charlie walked over to the mini bar and poured Nick and him a drink while Nick listened to his reasoning. "No," he continued, "he was looking for something. Trust me."

Nick took a gulp out of the glass when Charlie handed it to him. The bourbon burned his throat before warming his stomach when it landed.

"Thanks, Charlie." He told the detective that he now had a good deal of respect for. "Where do we go from here? Remember, we go to court for this on Thursday so I'd like to have something by then. You know, I think one friend from jail is enough. Why make it a habit?"

Charlie wasn't sure how to take that last part. "Well," he studied Nick, "I can't promise we'll have anything that soon but we'll start with me doing what you asked. Following Danny for awhile and checking into that girl he was with." He checked his notes to make sure Nick had given him the car's description and directions to the trailer park. He had. "Meanwhile I want you to search every inch of your basement. He was down there for a reason and I bet that that reason is still there. How does that sound?" Charlie finished his drink and set the empty glass back on the bar.

Nick stood up and set his glass next to Charlie's. "It sounds like you're hired, Charlie."

"Great," Charlie said as he looked at his watch. "Now I've got a couple of things to take care of this afternoon and evening so I'll be looking in on Danny starting first thing in the morning."

"Another big case?" Nick was disappointed. He had hoped Charlie would be able to start right away.

"Naw, just the usual. Another rich woman who thinks her big shot husband is cheating on her. I've got to stake out a motel, take some pictures, that sort of thing." Charlie saw Nick's disappointment. "Relax, Pal, you're in good hands. You just go on home and search that basement. I'll be in touch." He offered his hand.

"You know," Nick said as he shook Charlie's hand, "I had the wrong opinion of you at first. I want to say I'm sorry about that. I guess I do judge books by their covers."

Charlie smiled and walked over to his desk. He reached in a drawer and pulled out a scale model of the orange Charger from The Dukes of Hazzard '80's TV show and set it on the desk.

"I wouldn't worry about your investigative reporter instincts fading, Nick." Charlie told him. "They seem dead on."

Pam Roanik sat at her desk in the accounting firm she worked for, across town from where her husband was meeting with Charlie Tibbens. She was glad her boss was out of town because she had so much on her mind it kept her from concentrating on her job.

Why would Danny break in to the house? She wondered, staring at her blank computer screen. For that matter, what would he want out of the basement? You'd think the first place he'd go would be to his bedroom. I know how obsessive he is. It would make sense for him to want to make sure all of his possessions were intact.

Then again, she thought, maybe he did go to his bedroom first. Maybe he went through all the rooms first. Nick didn't know how long he'd been in there. Pam started to feel anxious. What if this also wasn't the first time he'd broken in there? Pam wondered why this didn't hit them both last night. They probably were just so shook up over the whole thing that the possibility of him doing it before never entered their minds. She decided to call home and let Nick know what she'd been thinking about. To tell him that maybe he should concentrate on looking over the whole house. Maybe Danny took care of whatever it was he went there for upstairs, then got nostalgic and went to the basement to masturbate by the furnace again. Stranger things have happened, she thought.

Pam picked up the phone and dialed her home number. When the answering machine clicked on she was disappointed. Nick hadn't told her that he had anything going on today. She assumed that he would be at home, fixing her sink. Maybe he's in the shower, she justified.

"Nick, honey," she spoke to the recording device, "I have some thoughts on what happened with Danny. Call me when you get this. Love you." Then she hung up.

While she waited for Nick to call back she was able to get a little work done. After about an hour the phone rang. Hoping it would be her husband she grabbed it after the first ring.

"Huntington and associates. Pam Roanik speaking. How can I help you?" She spoke into the receiver.

"Hi Pam Roanik." Jeff Nelson drew out the name Roanik sarcastically as he said it. "And how are you this afternoon?"

Pam rolled her eyes. "I'm a little busy Jeff, what do you want?"

"I need to see you. It's about Danny," Jeff told her.

Pam shot upright in her chair. "Danny!? What is it? Is he all right?" She bit her lip, hoping her son wasn't hurt.

214

"Well, he's okay at the moment but there's a problem. Can you come over here?" Jeff hoped he was expressing the right amount of concern.

"Why can't you just tell me what's going on?" She asked him.

"It's not something I want to get into over the phone. Besides, I think you need to see it first hand."

Pam thought she heard a muffled giggle from the other end of the line. "Jeff, if this is some sort of a joke…"

"Listen, Pam," Jeff interrupted, "This is serious. Your son, our son may be in some trouble. Now will you please come over here and talk with me about it?" Jeff was getting frustrated.

Trouble? Pam thought. Oh my god! Maybe he broke into another house. Or worse. "All right. I'm on my way." She stood up and grabbed her purse.

"Wait, Pam, There's more." Jeff took a breath. "He's acting strange. Violent outbursts and stuff. I don't know how he would react if he came home and saw your car in the drive. Would you mind parking it somewhere and taking a taxi? I don't want to upset him."

"What? All right, sure." Pam wasn't thinking straight now. Danny could definitely become violent at the drop of a hat. She'd seen that first hand. Besides, Jeff sure sounded worried, and he had spent the most time with Danny since this all began. Maybe the night he hit himself

215

was just the tip of the iceberg. She thought. Maybe he has gone over the deep end and really is dangerous, like Nick said. "I'll drive home and call a cab from there," she told him.

"Pam," Jeff yelled, "that's clear in the opposite direction. We don't have time to waste." He hoped she understood his sense of urgency. "Just find somewhere between your office and here to park. This is important and Danny will be home soon."

"All right, Jeff. I'm on my way," she said and hung up. Before she left she tried to reach Nick one more time to let him know what she was doing. When the answering machine picked up again she slammed the phone down without leaving a message. "Damn you Nick. Where the hell are you?" she fumed as she rushed out of her office.

Danny needed to think things over. That asshole Nick had screwed everything up, and in a big way. He couldn't sort things out sitting in the trailer with his dad. That just distracted him. Especially when every time he looked at Jeff all those horrible memories of the shed flooded his mind. Memories he needed to forget if he was going to make his plan work. If not forget, then at least push to the back of his mind for the time being. He had to stay focused.

Danny knew for sure that they hadn't found the

216

vase. That meant that whatever story Nick and Pam were

telling couldn't be confirmed. Danny knew the story they

were telling. The truth. He also knew that the truth was so

far fetched that no one could possibly believe it. Come on,

Danny thought, people don't just go around bashing

themselves in the face. Especially with a vase that no one

can prove even exists.

Danny almost let himself become engulfed in the

cleverness of his own scheme. Pretty soon Pam will start

her own version of the downward spiral that she put his

father on all those years ago. Nick on the other hand will

become happily married to some big guy named Bubba in

his new home at the penitentiary. At which time he won't

be able to ruin people's lives by spreading lies on

television. No, in there the only thing he'll be spreading is

his legs so Bubba can shove his cock further up Nick's ass.

Yeah, buddy!

Maybe it'll be safe over there. Danny thought about

his mom's house. After all, they didn't find the vase so I'm

sure they won't find that.

He finally decided that he should put all of it aside

for the day. Clear his mind for a while. I've worked hard

the last month or so and deserve a break, he reasoned. He

asked his dad if he could borrow a few bucks to see if Beth

wanted to go see a movie. He was actually surprised when

Jeff eagerly handed him twenty dollars. Didn't even give

me any of that get a job bullshit, Danny thought when he shoved the money in his pocket. Just told me to take as long as I wanted and then grinned, telling me to make sure to use part of the money to buy a condom.

That sort of made Danny uncomfortable but he thanked his dad anyway and went over to see if Beth was interested. She was, and to brighten Danny's day even more she also wanted to see the Bruce Willis movie. Not because of that, but because some guy named Colin Ferrill was in it as well. She said he was a "hottie." Danny didn't give a shit who this Colin guy was, or that he was hot, he was just glad to be going to a Bruce Willis movie with a pretty girl and enjoying himself again. He hadn't realized what a drain all of this was putting on him.

Pam drove in the direction of Jeff's trailer park. She was looking for a place to leave her car and was not satisfied with her choices. The strip heading to his place was not in the best part of town and consisted mainly of gas stations, fast food restaurants and motels. She decided against the first two simply because she didn't know how long she would be, and because they had signs up stating that it was parking for customers only and all others would be towed. So she decided that a motel lot would be the safest bet. They wouldn't know whether or not she was staying there or even if she was just visiting one of the guests.

She pulled into the parking lot of the next motel she saw and parked her car. She was so frazzled at this point, worrying about her son that she started to cry when she couldn't find her cell phone anywhere in her purse.

"I've got to get a damn taxi," she muttered, finally giving up the search and scanning the parking lot for a pay phone. Her eyes finally spotting one at the edge of the lot about ten feet away.

Pam grabbed her purse and locked the car. She ran to the phone and looked up a cab company in the torn phone book that was hanging underneath in a plastic cover.

"Hurry, Hurry." Her anxious voice quivered as she dropped in the coins and dialed.

"Red Line taxi service," came the deep voice at the other end. "How can we help you?"

"I need a taxi." Pam replied abruptly.

"Yes Ma'am. Just tell us where you want to get picked up and we'll be right out."

"I'm sorry, what?" Pam couldn't hear him that well because of all the traffic on the interstate nearby.

"Tell us where you're at and we'll get someone over there." The man said a little louder.

"Yes, yes of course. I'm at," Pam turned around to look at the neon sign shining from atop the motels' office and almost dropped the phone.

"You're where, Ma'am?" The dispatcher asked again when Pam didn't respond.

"I'm at the Mount Vernon Motel and Breakfast Nook." Pam said softly as she fell back against the door to the booth.

"Very well. Someone will be right over. Thank you." The dispatcher hung up.

Pam set the phone in the cradle and started to cry again. "I can't believe this," she whispered. "Of all the motels on this shitty strip I had to stop at this one. What was I thinking?"

She waited in the phone booth while she pulled herself together and was just about to try Nick again when the cab pulled in the parking lot. She looked at the cab and then back at the phone again. Jeff said it was urgent. She thought. I better go, I can call him from Jeff's house or tell him about it when I get home. Besides, I'll know more then anyway. Why worry him when I might not have to. He's stressed enough as it is.

Pam opened the door and walked over to the cab. When she got in she gave the driver Jeff's address. "Please hurry," she told him.

Nick got home that afternoon from his meeting with Charlie feeling good about things. He was planning on going down to the basement for a more thorough search right after he made himself a sandwich. He remembered that he hadn't eaten since breakfast, and bourbon on an empty stomach didn't agree with him. Even if it was only half of a glass.

On his way to the kitchen he pressed the answering machines' play button to hear his messages. Nick stopped when he heard the first one. It was from Pam.

I wonder what she came up with, he thought after hearing her mention Danny. The next and final message was just a hang up call. A very loud hang up call, Nick thought when he heard it.

When the machine shut off Nick picked up the receiver and called his wife's office to see what she wanted to tell him.

"You have reached the office of Pam Roanik. I'm away from my desk at..."

"Great, her voice mail," said Nick as he listened to the whole thing. When it came time for him to leave a message he told her that he was home and to call him. Then he went in the kitchen to make his sandwich.

Pam had the money ready when the taxi slowed in front of Jeff's trailer. She handed it to the driver and started walking towards the deck leading to the front door. As soon as the cab pulled away Jeff emerged from his shed.

"Pam thanks for getting here so fast." He looked up

and down the street. "Is Nick coming?" he asked cautiously.

"Nick? No, why? You said to hurry so I didn't get a chance to get a hold of him. Now what's going on? Where's Danny?"

Jeff did his best to hold in his grin. Good. He thought. No bastard Nick to deal with. "Come in here, I need to show you something. You're not going to believe what that kid did." Jeff pointed to the shed.

Pam looked from the shed to her ex-husband warily. What did Danny do? she thought. Practice for our house by breaking in to Jeff's precious little shed? "Is he all right?" she asked.

"Oh, he's fine." Jeff assured her while leading her in to the darkened shed.

Pam could smell the strong aroma of beer on his breath when she got closer to him.

"I can't see a thing in here Jeff." She turned to face him where the only light was the sun coming in from the door behind him. "Is there a light you can turn on?"

Jeff closed the door behind him and reached for the light switch. "Yeah, it's around here somewhere. Hold on."

"Jeff Nelson this isn't funny," Pam yelled at him through the blackness. "Open that door and tell me what's going on with our son, right now!" She was starting to have a bad feeling.

Jeff flipped on the light switch and through the grin he could no longer hide said, "Don't worry, Danny's fine. I just called you over here so I could have a little of what Ted Anders got."

Pam looked at him in horror. How did he know? Her mind raced. She took a step back as he came at her. "What do you think you're doing, Jeff? Let me out of here!"

Jeff laughed and kept coming closer. "Once a whore, always a whore. Right Pammy? How was it with Ted? Better than Nick?"

Pam didn't know what had gotten into Jeff, but she wasn't about to stick around and find out. She turned to look for something she could use to stop him and froze, a scream of terror forming in the pit of her stomach. Before she was able to get more than a short squawk out, she felt a hand slam over her mouth and nose holding a cloth, wet with something sweet smelling covering it. The last thing she saw before she passed out was an inflatable doll with a picture of her taped over its face and the word whore scrawled across its breasts.

"There, there, my little cheating slut," Jeff whispered in Pam's ear as her limp body fell against him, "you go ahead and go to sleep, it'll be just like old times." Then he reached over and tossed the doll on the floor and laid Pam on the cot in its place.

After he locked the door from the inside, Jeff turned back to Pam's sleeping body and started unbuttoning her blouse.

Nick finished his ham sandwich and started to head down to the basement to nose around when he thought he'd better try Pam's office again. When he went to pick up the phone something on the caller I.D. grabbed his attention. The number showing as the last number that called was Pam's office. Nick thought back for a minute. There was a call from Pam and then a hang up call on the answering machine. That was it. Their caller I.D. didn't show how many times a particular number called and it only listed the last time a particular number called you. Which means, if someone called the house from the same phone thirty times a day, the I.D. would constantly be updating and only the last call from that number would show up.

Knowing this began to worry Nick. That meant that Pam was the one who called and hung up. Loudly, he remembered. He had no way of knowing how much time passed between the first time Pam called with information about Danny and when she called and hung up. He did know that it had been an hour since he called her when he got home

Nick grabbed the phone and dialed her number. Again he got her voice mail. "Pam, call me as soon as you get this message," he said adamantly.

Nick was becoming more worried by the minute. It wasn't like his wife to just call and hang up without leaving a message. Especially after how excited she sounded the first time she called. He played the tape again. She said she thought of something concerning Danny, and then a call where the phone was slammed down. He listened to that on the tape again as well.

Something was definitely wrong here, Nick felt it. He dialed his wife's cell phone. When, after several rings he got that voice mail as well, Nick began to panic. Pam was a stickler about having her cell phone on. She was adamant about her children being able to reach her at any time. Nick knew that. He put the phone back and looked at the clock on the wall. It was 5:30, Pam got off work a half hour ago, he told himself, unless she had to stop at the store or something on the way home, she should be walking in the door any moment. Nick had a funny feeling she wouldn't. He sat down on the couch and tried to stay calm.

Meanwhile, across town in a motel parking lot, lying between the passenger seat and door of Pam Roaniks' car lay a cell phone with the red glow of a flashing light indicating an incoming message.

Another hour passed with no sign of Pam. Nick still tried not to think of the worst but with each passing minute it became clearer to him that something was wrong.

Maybe she stopped by the Anders house to visit with Sally, he thought. It's not like her to not let me know if she's going to be late, but it's possible she got over there and lost track of time. He hoped that's all it was when he picked up the phone to call Ted's house.

"Hi, Nick," Nora answered. "How are you guys holding up? Ted told me you've received a court date."

"What? Oh, yeah, Thursday." Nick told her. "Look Nora, is Pam over there by any chance?"

"Pam? No, actually Sally and I are the only ones home right now. Ted said he had to work late. Again," she sneered. "Why, is something wrong?" Nora sensed his concern.

"Probably not. She called from work earlier and left a message regarding Danny and I haven't been able to reach her since then."

"It's probably nothing, Nick, but since she mentioned Danny why don't you try over at his father's house? Maybe she stopped by there after work," Nora offered.

"Yeah," Nick kicked himself for not thinking of that himself, "that might be it. Thanks, Nora." Nick said before hanging up. On top of everything else, now he felt bad that he didn't even ask to say hello to Sally. Maybe she'll be able to come home Thursday and I can make it up to her,

226

Nick thought while thumbing through their phone listings for Jeff's number.

He hung up after the eighth ring went unanswered and started pacing the room. He also tried Pam's old friend Betty who also said she hadn't seen or heard from Pam. Nick's worry was escalating into panic now. By 8:00 he had tried the hospitals in the area where, to his relief, no one by the name of Pam Roanik or Jane Doe had been admitted that day. Three more unanswered attempts on her cell phone and Nick was at his wits end. The sickening feeling that had started small in the pit of his stomach was now growing at an alarming rate and Nick was powerless to stop it.

The clock on the mantle chimed 9:00. Where the hell are you? Nick wondered, staring at the phone, willing it to ring.

Charlie Tibbens sat in his car facing the Mount Vernon Motel and Breakfast Nook eating a burger and waiting. He had been sitting in the McDonald's parking lot across the street long enough to draw the attention of the manager who came out to check on him.

"We don't allow loitering sir. If your car won't start I have some jumper cables if you want?" the man asked helpfully but with a stern tone.

Charlie sucked down the rest of his Coke and

227

dismissed the man. "Who's loitering? I eat slow. Helps the digestion." Then he went back to his burger.

The manager shook his head and walked back in to the restaurant muttering. "Who takes two hours to eat a quarter pounder?"

Charlie sat in his car chewing on a french fry as he watched the manager pick up the phone in the restaurant and look through the window at him.

"Well," Charlie said as he wrapped up the rest of his sandwich and put it back in the bag with his fries, "I know that look. I guess it's time to move to a new location." Charlie figured the man was calling the police. On this side of town he would be stupid not to. For all he knows I'm casing his restaurant for a robbery. He started his car and turned out onto the busy strip and circled the block. He didn't want the manager to see him just cross the street, that would probably really make him paranoid.

Ten minutes later he eased in to the parking lot of the motel he had been watching. It was now getting dark and his eyesight wasn't what it used to be. He backed into a space by the pay phone at the corner of the lot and slid down in his seat. Mount Vernon Motel, he thought after surveying the place from his new spot, what a dive. Why do they always come to places like this, he asked himself,

Charlie did like cases like this. Easy money. Especially this one. Charlie didn't even have to do the leg work. The woman found a matchbook with the motel's name on it in her husband's suit coat. The same old story, he told her he had to work late. When she came to Charlie's office to see about hiring him she told Charlie that she didn't even confront her husband. She wanted proof before she went to him. Pictures. He wasn't going to have the chance to weasel out of this on a technicality. Charlie thought she seemed like a nice lady. Pretty too.

Charlie Tibbens had become hardened to the goings on between two adults. You have to, he thought, or you'll never last in this business. But it tore him up when children were involved. They're the ones that suffer the most when the adults can't keep their legs closed or their peckers holstered.

Charlie thought about the sweet little girl that came in with the woman that hired him. Very polite and well mannered. She sat in the waiting room coloring and singing while the adults went into his office to talk. He hoped for her sake that this was all just a big misunderstanding. He also knew from experience that it probably wasn't.

"Ow, shit!" Charlie reached down and rubbed his calf. "Damn cramp. That's the worst part of this kind of work." He looked around the parking lot and decided it was safe to get out and stretch for a minute.

Charlie hobbled around his car trying to work the cramp loose. Eventually the pain subsided and he was able to walk normally. He looked back at the cramped driver's seat and decided he could use a few more minutes of freedom. Looking around, he spotted a soda machine in the breezeway on the first floor and went over to it. After making his selection he pulled the tab open and leaned against the machine, taking a healthy gulp of the cold liquid. When he pulled the can from his lips he let out a belch and scanned the parking lot from his new angle.

"It's almost 9:00," he muttered, "I don't think this guy's going to show tonight." He took another swig from the can and started walking back to his car. "It's her money. I guess I can hang out a little bit longer."

Then he saw something that caught his attention. A vanity plate on the back of an Integra read ROANIK 2. Could be a coincidence, Charlie thought. Then again, how many people with the name Roanik could there be in these parts? It's not a common name around here. I think Nick said he was from up north somewhere. Charlie looked back at the motel and thought for a moment. He didn't like any of the scenarios that had begun to play out in his mind. He had come to like Nick Roanik and the thought that either him or his wife could be in this motel with someone else sickened and annoyed him.

The more he thought about it the madder Charlie got. Sure, there was the possibility that it was indeed a coincidence, but not likely. Charlie decided to find out.

He went back to his own car, the case he had been working on now taking a back seat to this whole Roanik issue. Charlie climbed in the seat and reached over to the passenger side for his briefcase. Inside he found Nick's number. When he pulled out his cell phone to dial, he stopped. Chances are very good, he thought, that the person who answers the phone over there is not going to like what I have to say. Hell, I don't even know his wife, is it my place to give her news like this if she's the one who picks up the phone?

Then another thought hit him. The car could have been stolen. Possibly even by the boy. If he'd break into their house without a second thought, then he very well could think nothing of "borrowing" their car.

Yes, he concluded, I've got to call them. At the very least they'll get a laugh that someone else in these mountains has the same last name as them. And at the most, Charlie looked at the phone in his hand, at the most, we'll see. Then he dialed the Roaniks' number.

"Hello, Pam?" a frantic sounding Nick answered before the first ring ended. He hadn't even taken the time to look at the caller I.D. before yanking up the receiver.

Charlie let out a sigh of relief when he heard Nick's voice on the other end. The relief quickly turned to sorrow for his friend at the thought of what this likely meant. "Nick, hi. It's me, Charlie. Charlie Tibbens."

"Charlie?" Nick was confused. "I'm kind of waiting on a phone call Charlie. Can you call me back tomorrow?" Nick choked.

"Nick, is everything all right? You sound funny."

"No, I have a bad feeling about Pam. She should have been home hours ago and I haven't heard from her. I'm worried something may have happened."

Charlie looked over at the Integra and slowly shook his head. He hated doing this. "Nick, I need to ask you one question. What kind of car does your wife drive?"

This took Nick by surprise. "An Acura Integra, why?"

Charlie swallowed hard. "What's the plate number?" He asked as calm as possible.

"It's a vanity plate, it says ROANIK 2, Charlie what are you leading up to? I told you I don't have time, my wife is missing." Nick snapped. "Now if you want to help, great, but otherwise I need to keep the phone clear."

"Nick," Charlie said softly, "I believe I've got some bad news for you."

CHAPTER X

Nick's SUV squealed into the Mount Vernon motel parking lot just fifteen minutes after hanging up the phone. He spotted Pam's car and pulled in beside it. Charlie came running over when he saw the determined look on Nick's face as he leapt from his SUV.

"Stay calm now, pal." Charlie tried to ease the situation. "Like I told you on the phone, we don't know for certain she's in there. I've been watching this place for most of the evening and this car has been here longer than me. I know because there were only three cars total when I arrived."

"It's been here all this time and you just now call me?" Nick glared at him.

"Well, yeah," Charlie put his hands in front of him palms up, I didn't see the plate to make the connection until I moved my surveillance over here from across the street."

"Fair enough." Nick rubbed the back of his neck and looked from the car to the motel then back to Charlie.

"I'm not sure I want to know the answers to the questions running through my mind."

Charlie didn't respond. He just followed his friend across the parking lot to the motel's office. A little bell above the door jingled as they came through, signaling a mousy little man with a handful of hair pasted across his forehead.

"You fellows' in need of a room?" he asked from behind the counter.

"Not tonight. I'm looking for a woman," came Nick's reply.

The desk clerk's beady eyes shifted between the two men in front of him. "Um, Sir, this isn't that kind of an establishment."

Nick slammed his fist on the counter so hard the little man let out a scream and began reaching for the phone. Charlie pulled his friend back and walked around the counter. He placed his hand on top of the quivering clerk's and gently but firmly helped the man ease the phone back into its cradle. Charlie then produced a twenty dollar bill and placed it on the counter beside him.

"Take a breath there, big guy." Charlie told him. "We aren't looking for trouble, just some information." The clerk looked at Charlie, then at the money that lay beside him. He couldn't muster the nerve to look at Nick, although he felt the man's glare. "What kind of information?" he asked.

"We want to know if you have a woman staying here by the name of Pam Roanik," Charlie told him.

"That name doesn't ring a bell but I'll check." The man eased past Charlie and started going through his registration records. "No, no Pam Roanik. Sorry."

"This is bull shit!" Nick was back at the counter again. "If she was in a place like this, which I doubt she ever would be, she sure as hell wouldn't use her real name." Nick flung out his wallet and tossed a picture of Pam across the counter for the man to look at. "Now, is she here?"

The clerk ran his hand across his forehead to replace the hairs that had become unglued and were by this time sliding down his sweaty face into his eyes. Then he picked up the picture and studied it.

"Yes," he said finally. "Yes, I've seen her."

Nick and Charlie looked at each other. "So she *is* here?" Charlie asked.

"Oh, no," replied the clerk. "I saw her when she arrived. I thought she was going to get a room but I guess she just stopped because she had car trouble."

"Why do you say that?" Nick questioned.

"Well, she never even came in the office. She got out of that car there," he pointed at the Integra in the lot, "then she went to the pay phone, a little while later a taxi pulled up and she got in it."

"Where was she going?" Nick demanded.

"How would I know? But judging from the fact that she was crying off and on, and your temper, sir, she was probably going someplace you weren't." The clerk sniffed.

At that point Charlie had to physically remove Nick from the office before he killed the little man. When they got outside, the desk clerk came around the counter and locked the door. On his way back he slipped the twenty dollar bill into his pocket.

"This doesn't make any sense, Charlie." Nick shook his head as they approached Pam's car. "If she were going to cheat on me, why go through all of this. No, she's in trouble. I know it."

"Sounds like it to me, too. I'm sorry to say." Charlie agreed. "Maybe we should call the police."

Nick stopped in his tracks. "No police. Not yet anyway. Think about it. They've all ready charged me with domestic violence and now my wife comes up missing. Who do you think is going to be the prime suspect? Me, that's who. They'll waste valuable time locking me up and questioning me for hours. Time that we may not have. Time Pam may not have. Charlie, I know my wife. She wouldn't just leave. Not without calling. Something's happened to her. Will you help me?" Nick was pleading. He was truly scared.

"I'll do everything I can," Charlie promised him. "Let's start there. Do you have a spare key?" he asked, pointing at Pam's car.

Nick had the key out and was sprinting the rest of the distance to the car. The key was in the door before Charlie caught up to him. Nick opened the driver side door and pushed the power lock button so Charlie could get in the passenger side. When Charlie opened it he saw the red flashing light of Pam's phone. He reached down, picked it up and handed it to Nick.

When Nick took it he felt light headed. He flopped down in the driver's seat and took a breath. Playing back the incoming messages didn't give them any answers. The only calls on there were from Nick himself.

Pam, Nick thought, where are you, baby? He looked around for Charlie and saw that he was standing by the pay phone writing in a note pad with the phone cradled between his shoulder and ear. Nick walked over as Charlie hung up.

"There are too many cab companies around here to waste time calling them all," he turned and said to Nick. "So I did a little bluffing with Ma Bell and we got lucky."

"What do you mean?" Nick was feeling hopeful.

"Well, I called the phone company and told them I lost..." Charlie began.

"Not your life story, what do you mean we got lucky?" Nick insisted.

"Well, to make a long story short, the last call made from this phone was to Red Line Taxi service. So I thought, what are the odds? I gave them a call and…"

"And what? What did you find out?" Nick couldn't take it anymore.

"If you'll stop interrupting me I'll tell you," Charlie said. "As I was saying, it turns out that they did have a cab dispatched to this motel today. And luckily for us, it was only one cab and the driver picked up a woman fitting Pam's description."

Nick, still worried, but getting more hopeful, dared ask one last question. "Did they remember where the destination was?" He prayed.

"Yes, to a trailer park a couple of miles from here, called…" Charlie looked at his notes.

He didn't need to bother. Nick was already racing for his car. "That son of a bitch!" he yelled.

"Nick wait!" Charlie yelled as he chased after him. "I'll drive. You try to reach them on the cell phone."

"Okay, but hurry!" Nick panted. "I don't know what the hell is going on, but whatever it is I have a feeling it's not good." Nick tossed the keys to Charlie and jumped into the passenger seat. He had the phone out and was ready to dial when Charlie started up the engine.

"What's wrong?" Charlie asked him while he backed out of the parking space. "Dial the number."

Nick sat there and stared at the phone in his hand. "I can't. I just realized that I don't know the number," he told Charlie, suddenly feeling defeated.

"What do you mean you don't know the number?" Charlie took his eyes off of the road and stared at Nick in disbelief.

"Quit looking at me that way. It's written down in a book at home. I never bothered to memorize it, okay? I never thought I'd be calling my wife's ex-husband in the first place, so why would I need to?" Nick said, but at the same time he was scolding himself for not knowing it.

"Well, try your house then." Charlie was trying anything he could think of to keep his new friend's mind occupied. "Maybe she called since you left. You can get your messages that way can't you? She might even be there by now," he offered, but didn't believe it. Why would she go home without picking up her car first?

Nick didn't think of that. A glimmer of hope crossed his face as he dialed his house. The glimmer didn't last long. It faded the second he heard the mechanical voice tell him there were no new messages.

"Which trailer is it?" Charlie asked as he turned in to the park.

Nick looked around for a second. "That one. Fifth one on the left." Charlie pulled in the gravel driveway and before he could put the vehicle's transmission in park Nick was out the door, running up the steps of the trailer. He was banging on the screen door when Charlie caught up to him.

"There are no lights on." Charlie noticed after Nick's pounding had become an effort in futility. "Maybe they went somewhere?" he offered.

"Then we'll wait." Nick determined. "They can't stay gone forever." He looked around the deck for a place to sit. "Wait a minute. Do you hear that?" he asked.

The two of them stood there quietly, straining to hear what sounded like faint music playing.

"Sounds like a radio playing somewhere," Charlie said.

Nick went down the steps and cocked his head to get a better feel for where the music was coming from. It wasn't from inside the trailer, he decided. The two of them looked towards the trailer next to Jeff's and a thought hit Charlie.

"It might be coming from them," he suggested. "Let's go over and find out. Even if it's not, maybe they saw something that might clear this up."

They started walking across the lawn but both stopped before they got to the next trailer. "I can't hear it anymore," Nick said. "It was barely audible before but now I can't hear it at all, can you?"

The two of them stood in the grass on the neighbor's side of the property line and strained their ears.

"No, I can't hear it either," Charlie told him and started walking slowly back towards Jeff's place. He stopped when he reached the shed. "Come here, listen," he whispered to Nick.

When Nick came over they both put their ear to the side of the shed and listened. The music, while still faint, was definitely coming from inside. They heard something else, too. Also faint, but slightly louder than the music, they heard what sounded like moaning.

Charlie looked at Nick and saw hurt flush over his face. The look quickly turned to anger and Nick clenched his fists and walked determinedly to the door of the shed.

Charlie was right beside him. Neither of them knew for sure what they would find on the other side, but both had their suspicions. Charlie wanted to be close in case he had to stop his friend from making a big mistake.

Nick quietly tried the door knob with a shaking hand. If his wife was screwing her ex, he thought, he was damn sure not going to give them the courtesy of knocking. When he found that the door was locked, he had had enough. Nick looked over at Charlie, stepped back and kicked the door so hard that it flew open, hit the wall and bounced back. Nick smacked it open again and rushed into the shed.

What Nick was now staring at was so horrific that it would give him nightmares for the rest of his life. He was

241

both shocked and repulsed. There, lying on a cot in the corner was his wife, naked except for a deflated blow-up doll tied around her neck. On top of her, also naked, Jeff Nelson was furiously pumping inside her, oblivious to Nick and Charlie's presence. His lips seemed glued to Pam's as her lifeless eyes stared blankly toward the ceiling, bulging from their sockets.

It took Nick a split second to leap towards them and yank Jeff off of her, throwing him like a rag doll against the wall.

"Pam, no!" Nick yelled as he loosened the blow-up doll from his wife's neck.

Charlie grabbed Jeff and held him from behind while fighting the urge to vomit at what he'd just witnessed. "You sick bastard!" he growled into Jeff's ear while Nick was desperately trying to breathe air in to Pam's lungs, tears streaming down his face.

Then they heard a scream. Charlie and Jeff looked to the door and saw Danny and Beth standing there. Danny went numb as his eyes went from his mom's body, to his dad, who was staring glassy eyed at Pam. Danny looked at his naked father up and down then his eyes froze on something and it all sunk in. It was all true. He started to vomit. Beth saw what Danny was looking at and started screaming even louder.

Nick was unaware of everything going on around

him as he tried to resuscitate his wife, but Charlie looked over Jeff's shoulder and saw it too. Jeff was so entranced watching Nick give mouth to mouth to Pam's naked body that he had a trail of spittle hanging from the corner of his mouth. But that wasn't what caused Danny to vomit, or Beth to scream louder, or even cause Charlie to let go of his grip on Jeff in revulsion. No, all that was caused by the fact that not only did Jeff still have an erection, but he was playing with it as well.

"Call 911!" Charlie was finely able to muster the words. "Get an ambulance and the cops out here. Now!" His voice shook Danny back to his senses. He grabbed Beth's hand and pulled her into the trailer and made the call.

Jeff slid against the wall all the way down to the floor and started muttering something. Charlie wanted to squeeze his neck until Jeff's head burst open when he saw the little puddle of semen lying on the floor at the head of his penis. The only thing that stopped him was when he bent over close enough to get his hands on him; he was able to hear what Jeff was mumbling.

"I just wanted a little of what Ted Anders got." Jeff whispered over and over again.

Charlie went cold. He looked over at Nick and felt sick to his stomach. He not only didn't have the heart to tell Nick what he had just heard, he didn't see any point in it.

What would it change? He stayed like that, watching his friend as he cradled his dead wife's head in his arms until the sound of sirens filled the shed.

When the police arrived Charlie told them what had happened while the paramedics tended to Pam. When they determined that there was nothing that could be done they tried to help the people that seemed to need it the most. They gave a near hysterical Beth a shot to calm her down enough for the police to get her statement and then looked to Nick.

"What kind of person would do this?" Nick asked numbly as he stood in the corner staring at the progression of pictures around the walls. He handed one of them the blow-up doll and walked out of the shed, unable to take anymore.

Outside wasn't any better. A crowd of Jeff's neighbors were being held back by police while other officers were securing the crime scene. Jeff Nelson sat in the back of one of the patrol cars now wearing a pair of shorts and a T-shirt that Danny had gotten from the trailer at an officers request.

Nick watched in silence as the ambulance carrying his wife's body drove off. No lights, no sirens, no reason to hurry, he thought as he sat there and cried. He didn't even see the officer approaching him.

"Mr. Roanik? I'm sorry for your loss, and I know

this isn't the best time but I have a couple of questions I need to ask if you're up to it?" The officer sat down next to Nick.

Nick looked at the officer for a second then went back to staring at the ground. "I'll do my best." He sighed.

"Well," the cop took out his notes, "most of it can wait for now. We got quite a bit from Mr. Tibbens over there." He pointed at Charlie who was talking to another officer. "He says the two of you arrived together looking for your wife who hadn't come home from work. Is that correct?"

"Yes."

"And when you arrived, she was," the officer paused to try to think of a delicate way to say it, "um, already deceased?"

Nick turned away and started shaking. "I don't know. I think so. I tried giving her mouth to mouth but she wouldn't wake up."

The cop decided he'd pushed enough for tonight. They had their suspect. They could afford to let this man grieve. He had to ask the next question though.

"Mr. Roanik I just have one more question for tonight. Due to the boy's father being in custody and his mother, well," he paused and looked towards Danny, "we need to know if you know of any place he can stay tonight." The cop hoped this would be easy. Surely the man would want his wife's son to stay with him, wouldn't he?

That was the last straw for Nick. He turned to the cop, wiped the tears from his eyes and stood up. "I'll tell you where he can go, to hell, that's where!" Nick was getting loud and didn't care who heard him. "It's his fault all this happened! If it weren't for all his lies my wife would still be alive. You know what? I know the perfect place for him to live, call Ann Randall at D.S.S. He loves them so much and she knows everything there is to know about raising kids. I think they'd be a perfect match." Then Nick turned and walked off to his car while the police, Charlie, the crowd that had gathered, and even Danny watched in disbelief.

He drove out of the trailer park just as his old news team was pulling in. The thought of his wife's murder and rape being flashed all over the area via television would have made him sick if he didn't realize at that moment, sadly, that months ago he would be the one racing to be the first on the scene. Months ago, in another life, another Nick.

As Nick pulled away, Danny overheard one cop tell another to get someone from D.S.S. out there. "Shit," he said under his breath. "I'm fucked now. Why didn't that asshole Nick just tell them he would take me in? What did I ever do to him?"

CHAPTER XI

On Thursday morning Nick was just going through the motions. He hadn't slept since Pam died. In fact, he hadn't done much of anything since Pam died. That is except cry until there were no tears left, and try to make sense of it all. Try to understand how in a few short months they had gone from a happy family to his wife being murdered.

He had court that morning but the outcome of that was the farthest thing on his mind. He drove to the courthouse in a daze. Unshaven and unkempt he went through the metal detectors and up to the eighth floor to the juvenile court room.

When his lawyer, Ted Anders spotted him he rushed right over. He had been trying to get in touch with Nick since he heard the news about Pam.

"Nick." Ted took his friend's arm and led him into a quiet corner. "I'm so sorry about Pam. If there is anything on a personal level I can do for you, just let me know."

Ted looked at his friend and thought about the last time he had seen Pam. He felt a twinge of pain in his groin but even that didn't make him believe she did enough to deserve to die. He realized that day as he lay on the couch in his office, slipping in and out of consciousness, that it was he that had been in the wrong, not Pam. Ted knew he deserved everything she did to him, and he hated that he would never have the chance to tell her.

He cleared his throat when Nick didn't respond. "I'm going to ask for the judge to dismiss the charges against you today. If that doesn't work, I'm sure he'll grant us a continuance." Ted paused and turned his eyes away from Nick. "Considering the circumstances," he finished softly.

Nick just nodded absently, his mind somewhere else.

While Nick was in a fog as he prepared for the days proceedings, Danny was pacing his room at the county group home where he had spent the time since his mother's murder. He didn't know who had lied to him more, his mother or his father. He couldn't erase the image burned in his mind of his dad's glazed look as he masturbated to the sight of his dead ex-wife. He didn't want to think about what was probably going on in that shed just minutes before Beth and he arrived. Danny shivered as he paced. He shivered because deep down he knew what was going on. His dad did fuck dead people. The police had been right. The newspaper had been right. But most of all, his mother and Nick had been right.

Danny did what everyone whose mind had come to

the point of sensory overload did. He buried the thoughts.
He pushed every bit that he could as far back into the deep
recesses of his mind as possible. He did a good job, too. In
time even the image of his father's self gratification reared
its ugly head less and less until it would only show up in
the darkness of his dreams. But that would be in time, not
today. Today it blazed through Danny's head like a neon
billboard.

"Come on Danny, it's time to go." Justine
Woodward knocked at his door.

Danny stopped pacing and glared at the door.
Although he was grateful for the distraction, he was
irritated by the fact that his plan had gone sour and now he
had to live like a prisoner at the group home. Or do I, he
thought.

He only had a few months to go until his eighteenth
birthday and he was damn sure he was not going to spend it
in some D.S.S. group home with a bunch of losers. Even
though Nick had refused to take me in, he told himself, I
still have options other than this. I have rights.

Danny climbed in the car beside Justine and listened
to what felt like the hundredth time to him someone telling
him how sorry they were to hear about his mother. Don't
these people understand I lost a father as well? No matter
how despicable what he did was, he's still my father,
Danny thought.

When the two of them walked into the court room Danny spotted Nick right away. He was standing in a corner with that Anders guy. Danny looked his step-father over and couldn't believe his appearance. He couldn't remember Nick ever letting himself go like this. Even when he'd take a weeks vacation and they'd go to the beach he always looked impeccable.

Danny didn't think Nick knew he was there. In fact, judging from the distant look in his eyes, he didn't think Nick knew anybody was there.

"All rise," came the bailiff's voice. "The honorable Judge Randolph presiding."

"Be seated." Judge Randolph motioned for the first case.

"The Department of Social Services verses Nick Roanik in the matter of juvenile Daniel Nelson," announced the clerk. "All parties involved please come forward."

Ted eased Nick to the defense table on the left side of the court room. Ann Randall sat with the attorney for D.S.S. at the prosecution table on the right, while Justine pointed Danny to the Guardian Ad Litem table between the two.

The charges against Nick for abuse and neglect were read and Nick was able to stand and whisper 'not guilty' to the court. Then Ted Anders asked the Judge to dismiss the charges due to the lack of tangible evidence against his client and that the prosecution's entire case revolved around the word of a teenager with history of delinquent behavior.

The prosecution's rebuttal to this was that every child, even ones with histories of delinquent behavior deserves his chance to be heard. After all, haven't studies shown that the majority of teenagers who break the law are acting out in aggression towards something in their home life?

While all this was going on, Nick sat in his chair absently turning a pencil in his hands, oblivious to what was being said. Judge Randolph listened to the prosecutor and decided that the case would be heard. Ann Randall smirked triumphantly at Ted when the Judge gave his ruling.

Ted Anders didn't give up. "Then if it pleases the court," he started, "the defense asks that you grant us a continuance in this matter due to the devastating loss my client suffered just two days ago."

The judge looked at Nick. Noticing how lost he looked he asked both council to approach the bench. "What loss are you referring to, Mr. Anders?" he asked when they both arrived.

"My client found his wife murdered on Tuesday evening, your Honor. As if that wasn't enough, at the time he found her deceased body, it was being sexually assaulted by her ex-husband. I feel my client needs a respectable amount of time to grieve and come to terms with the atrocity of his loss."

As Ted's words started to sink in, the prosecutor stared at him in horror and began to gag. Judge Randolph, though equally disgusted at what he just heard held his composure and waved the bailiff to bring the prosecutor some water.

"I take it by that response, Mr. Prosecutor; you have no objection to a continuance?" the Judge asked him.

"None whatsoever, your Honor," the man managed to gasp.

"Very well, we'll reconvene on this matter two months from today," the Judge declared as the attorneys took their seats. "Is there any thing else regarding this case that needs to be dealt with today?"

"There is one other matter we would like to address your Honor." Ted stood up. "The matter of Sally Nelson. My clients' step-daughter. Due to the loss of both her biological mother and father, and the fact that D.S.S. has offered no evidence to show of any abuse or neglect on the part of my client and the child, we beg the court to do the only humane thing possible in this case and return custody of Sally Nelson back to my client so the family can grieve together."

For the first time in days Nick seemed to respond. At the mention of Sally he looked around the court room and up at the Judge. Judge Randolph caught this and asked the prosecution if they had any evidence to show that Sally would be in danger if placed back in her home.

Ann Randall flipped through her notes furiously as the D.S.S. lawyer looked at her.

"Mr. Prosecutor?" the judge asked again. "Can you show me any reason not to let the girl be returned to her family?"

The D.S.S. lawyer looked at Ann who shook her head, seething. "No your Honor," he told him. "We've not seen any evidence to show that the girl would be harmed if placed back in Mr. Roanik's custody."

"Very well then," began the Judge, "Mr. Roanik, effective immediately you are Sally Nelson's legal guardian."

Nick slumped over in his chair and began sobbing. He hadn't lost everything. He would honor his wife's memory by raising Sally as he'd known Pam would want. "Thank you your Honor. Thank you so much," he was able to say between sobs.

Judge Randolph managed a smile for the man in front of him who had the misfortune of witnessing one of, if not the most heinous act a person can do to another person. Let alone a loved one. He turned back to the other matter at hand.

"What does the Department recommend regarding the custody and placement of Daniel Nelson?" Judge Randolph asked.

Ann Randall stood up. The Department requests that the minor remain in our custody with placement at the County Foster Care Group Home until this matter is settled or his eighteenth birthday, whichever comes first."

Shit! thought Danny. I'd better do something fast or I'm going to be stuck with those orphaned bed wetters for months.

Danny stood up. "Your honor?" he asked in his most polite voice. "May I say something on my own behalf?"

All eyes were on Danny, even Nick's. Like watching a train wreck, or an accident on the freeway, he couldn't wait to hear what line of shit the boy was going to try to feed the court.

"Go right ahead, son," Judge Randolph said.

"Well this is kind of hard. In front of all these people, I mean." Danny lowered his eyes to the table in front of him.

"Would you feel more comfortable in my chambers, young man?" the Judge offered.

"I, I don't want to take that much of your valuable time, your Honor." Danny looked up at him. "But if it wouldn't be too much trouble?"

"Certainly, Daniel." The Judge smiled at him. "I call a thirty minute recess. Council, Guardian, my chambers please."

"What the hell is he up to now?" Nick asked Ted.

"I guess I'm about to find out. Go get some air, Nick, and maybe some coffee. Be back here in this chair in twenty minutes." Ted told him and then got up to go to Judge Randolph's chambers.

Justine Woodward sat in the gallery and shook her head in disgust. Does this kid have no conscience whatsoever, she thought. His mother is murdered, his father is in jail for that murder and he's still working some angle to benefit himself.

"Sit down gentlemen." The Judge pointed the three adults to the couch against the back wall. "Daniel, have a seat." He led Danny to the chair in front of his mahogany desk. "Now, young fellow, what is it you'd like to say."

Danny shuffled his feet and avoided the Judges eyes. "I was embarrassed to say this in front of her and all those people out there, your Honor." He paused for effect. "I just don't feel comfortable staying at the group home, sir."

"Why, Daniel?" The Judge asked as all in the room listened intently.

"Well, your honor, it's Ms. Randall. Don't get me

wrong she's a nice lady. She really helped me out in the beginning."

"Go ahead," urged the Judge.

Danny took a deliberate breath. "And I never had a problem with her when I was staying with my father." Danny stopped. He was obviously uneasy, looking over his shoulder at the lawyers and guardian staring at him.

"It'll be all right." The Judge encouraged him.

"Well, it's just that, now that she has access to me all day long," he paused again, "and all night, she's been doing things that make me uncomfortable. Things that seem wrong, make me feel dirty." Danny looked up at the Judge and pleaded. "Please don't make me stay there! I don't want her touching me in that way anymore!" he begged. "Let me stay at my father's trailer. I'm all most eighteen. I can lock the doors to keep her away from me!"

When the shock of what they all just heard wore off, the D.S.S. prosecuting attorney jumped off of the couch. "Your Honor! Are we to believe that Ann Randall, a well respected employee at D.S.S. for several years, with a spotless record I might add, is molesting this boy?"

"See!" Danny started crying. "I knew no one would believe me. Haven't I been through enough? First I'm beat at home, then my father kills my mother, and now I'm supposed to lie back and let the only people that are supposed to be there for me make me perform for them sexually?"

"Your Honor, please!" the prosecutor charged. "Don't tell me you actually believe all this."

"Sit down Mr. Prosecutor," Judge Randolph snapped. "Daniel, this is a very serious accusation you're making against Ms. Randall. Are you sure you want to accuse her of sexual abuse?"

"Yes, your honor." Danny sniffed. "Let me stay at my father's house. Where she can't get to me."

Ted sat back, mildly amused. He'd seen this act before. The prosecutor, on the other hand, was livid. "Your Honor," began the D.S.S. lawyer, "this is ridiculous, this kid is lying."

"Mr. Prosecutor," Judge Randolph glared, "did you not object to the defense's request to dismiss this case partially on the grounds that 'every child deserves his chance to be heard?"

"Yes sir, but this…" came the reply.

"Then let's give this child the benefit of the doubt. If he claims he's being molested by Ms. Randall, then it's our duty to look into the validity of the claim." The Judge turned his attention back to Danny. "Son, I'm not at liberty to allow minors to live on their own, especially at a residence that is currently a crime scene. However, I order you to stay at the county group home where for your safety," he looked back at the D.S.S. lawyer, "Ann Randall will be placed on administrative leave pending an investigation. In addition, she is to have no contact with this child during this time. Gentlemen that is my order." He then smiled at Danny as he came around the desk and patted his shoulder. "If you have any more problems, son, you just let me know." The Judge then led the group back into the court room to announce his decision.

Danny walked back to his seat at the Guardian Ad Litem table feeling stunned. How the hell did that back fire? I had him. In the palm of my hand, I had him, he thought.

Ann Randall appeared just as upset as Danny. Some of her co-workers had to escort her from the court room when her outbursts at hearing what the judge had ordered almost got her a contempt charge.

Justine Woodward, on the other hand, had to cover her mouth when her boss passed by to keep Ann from seeing her laughing at the audacity of Danny. The little shit was good, she thought, real good.

As Judge Randolph tried to regain order in his court room, Danny showed no sign of defeat as he glared at Ann during her tirade. At the defense table, Ted smiled and slapped his friend on the back, telling Nick that it was all going to work out fine.

ONE MONTH LATER

Nick Roanik had settled back into his routine as best he could. He missed Pam dearly but was able to find happiness in the eyes of the nine year old girl he was now raising. Sally was adjusting too. She was glad to be back home with Nick, but sometimes he would see her face turn sad when she would look at one of the many pictures of her mother that Nick still was not ready to put away. Not only did seeing them help him through his grief, but they helped keep Pam alive in Sally's eyes. Nick would always stop whatever he was doing when Sally looked that way and he would pull her onto his lap and tell her stories reminding her of how much her mother loved them.

On this particular afternoon Sally had a friend over to play with. The friend kept her company and allowed Nick some time to get a few things done around the house. As he was sweeping out the basement he caught the furnace out of the corner of his eye. He leaned the broom against the wall as a thought occurred to him. So much had happened since that day. The day he'd found Danny in the basement and the girl in his driveway. So many sad, hurtful things, he thought.

Nick had forgotten all about it. Now, though, as he stood in the doorway of the laundry room and stared at the

259

furnace, it all came back to him. Danny was after something down here that day, he reminded himself.

Nick walked over to the furnace and looked around it, top to bottom. He slowly circled the metal structure wondering what could be so interesting about it that a boy had to stop whatever he was doing to play with himself beside it. And what, he wondered, was so important that that same boy would risk so much to come back for it?

After the third time around it, Nick leaned against the furnace frustrated. He stared at the concrete wall behind it and tried to come up with an answer. Directly in front of him, in the concrete was a metal door about the size of a fuse box, flush with the wall. Nick knew the door. It was the door to the box that held all the ashes from the fireplace in the living room above. Nick remembered the old house in Michigan where he grew up had the same sort of thing. As he looked at it he remembered how after every couple of fires he was supposed to take the shovel and scrape all the ashes down through the bottom of the fireplace in to a chute that dropped them all in a box like this one. Then, once a year or so he was supposed to shovel all the ashes that had built up in the box over the winter into a trash can to be hauled away. He remembered his father telling him that that was his job each winter.

Nick hated that job. Michigan winters were harsh and his family was no different than most up there in that they used the fireplace a lot. Nick laughed as he remembered how when Pam and he bought this house he told her that the job of scraping the ashes would now be passed down to Danny. After all, isn't that what fathers do? Pass down the chores that they can't stand doing to their sons, all in the name of building character.

Nick also remembered feeling slightly ripped off in the passing of the shitty job torch to Danny. North Carolina winters are nothing compared to Michigan ones. In fact there had been some years here, he thought, that they didn't use the fireplace at all. Nick tried to remember the last time they had used it when it hit him.

Nick pushed himself forward off of the furnace and grabbed the little metal latch that held the door closed. He opened the door and looked inside the dark, dusty space. Unable to see any thing he reached his hand in and felt around. Feeling nothing at first, he ran his hand across the bottom and heard the distinct sound of rustling plastic. He curled his fingers across his find and slowly slid out what appeared to be a composition book sealed inside of a Zip-Lock bag.

"Well, what do we have here?" Nick whistled as he shook the dust and thin layer of ash from the plastic.

He opened the bag and slid out a black imitation leather book and opened it. When he started reading what was written in Danny's handwriting he began to shake.

Nick needed to sit down. Without bothering to close the metal door or pick up the Zip-Lock bag he had dropped, he crossed the basement and went upstairs.

Sitting down on the couch Nick took a few deep breaths, opened the journal again and thumbed through it. Inside were lists, itineraries and descriptions of things. Most of it was things Nick didn't understand. Things like 'get Mr. Farly's computer code' and 'access child porn'. A few pages later there was something about a needing a bag of marijuana for some back pack. Keep in closet floor until needed, it said next to an asterisk. None of this made any sense to Nick. None of it until he got to a page labeled 'revenge on mom.'

The first two items listed under that heading were the telephone numbers to D.S.S. and Channel 9 news.

Nick set the book beside him and took a breath. He thought back to the night he was arrested. He remembered that when Ted bailed him out there were reporters all over the place. Neither Ted nor he could figure out how they got the story so fast. Now he knew.

He stood up and slowly walked down the hall to Danny's old room. Still just the way he left it. Nick opened the closet door and looked down at the floor inside. Squatting down on one knee he felt around the floor boards. When he came across one that felt loose he paused. Nick knew what he would find underneath even before he lifted the floor board out.

Nick pried the board loose and looked inside the space underneath. He had been right. He reached in and pulled out the vase that they had been looking for since that night. Standing up, he held it in the light and turned it in his hand. He stopped turning it when he got to the side with Danny's dried blood caked to it. Nick sat on the bed and gingerly touched the spot of blood, watching as parts of it flaked off and fell into his lap.

"This is all I need," he said to himself quietly. "This and that journal are all I need to clear my name."

But then what, he thought. There's no way I can go back to being a news man. I've seen too much. Felt too much of what the other side feels to be able to do that again with a clear conscious.

Nick thought again about how humiliated and degraded he felt leaving the jail and having his face plastered over every television in western North Carolina. Knowing that people were sitting comfortably in their living rooms, quietly judging him.

He remembered, too, his anger at seeing the reporter rodeo rushing to be the first to tell everyone about his wife's murder. No, Nick couldn't stomach the thought of doing that to another person again. He set the vase on Danny's night stand and turned the bloody side towards the wall. Nick then left the room, closing the door behind him.

When Nick got back to the living room he noticed
that Sally and her friend had come in and were in the
middle of a board game.

"Having fun sweetie?" he asked her.

"We sure are, dad. Can Darlene and I have
something to drink?" she asked.

"Sure Honey, there's some pop in the 'fridge." Nick
told her. When he sat back down on the couch he couldn't
help but smile when he heard Darlene ask Sally what 'pop'
was.

"Oh, he's from up north. That's what they call soda.
I don't get it either." Nick heard Sally answer her friend.

Leaning back, Nick picked up the journal from
where he had left it and opened it up again. He started
reading about Danny's plan to make Pam suffer for the hurt
and humiliation she had caused his father. Nick turned the
page and found out that his plan had meant for Sally and
Danny both to live with Jeff in order to make his mom feel
the same sense of complete loss that Jeff told him Pam
caused.

Nick closed his eyes and thought; I hope you can
sleep at night, Danny. I hope your mother's death was
worth it to you to help your father. He looked over at Sally,
back playing her game, and thought of how Danny's selfish
plan worked out better than he imagined. You caused a lot
more people than just your mom to feel a complete loss. He

thought.

The phone ringing pulled Nick out of his thoughts. "Hello," he said into the receiver.

"Mr. Roanik?" came the woman's voice on the other end. "This is Ann Randall, from D.S.S. calling. I was wondering if I could talk to you for a minute."

Great, Nick thought, what now? "It's not really a good time, Ms. Randall, I'm kind of busy." Nick lied.

"This really won't take long," she pushed, "I just wanted to ask for your help on something."

"You want *my* help?" Nick was puzzled. "On what?"

"Well, you heard in court what Danny is trying to accuse me of." Ann began. "I think we both know it's not true."

"How do we know that," Nick's tone sneered sarcasm. "Have we done studies on the likelihood of social workers to molest children in their custody?"

Ann ignored the remark. "What I was getting at, Mr. Roanik," she said as sweetly as she could. Like it or not, she needed this man and she knew it. "You had said something in the past about Danny having some sort of emotional problems, O.C.D. I think it was. Anyway, I want you to testify on my behalf about some of the behavior you've witnessed in Danny. That his emotional well being is unstable. Would you do that for me, Mr. Roanik? This is my career we're talking about here."

Nick thought for a moment. He really wanted to put this whole thing behind him and move forward. He looked over at the journal lying next to him and thought how the stuff written inside would easily clear both his name as well as Ann's. He didn't much like the idea of helping the woman who had him sent to jail based solely on some studies they had done regarding step parents, but he was tired. Tired, and ready to start anew. He had been angry for months now and it's gotten him nowhere. Nick looked over at Sally and felt it was time to put the past behind them and get on with their lives.

Nick smiled as the girls giggled over their game and was about to answer Ann Randall's question when he heard Darlene ask Sally if she wanted to spend the night at her house.

Sally got a scared look on her face when she told her friend, "I don't spend the night at other peoples' houses anymore."

"Why not?" her friend quizzed.

"Because once you get over there you're not allowed to come back home for a long, long time," Sally told her sadly.

When Nick heard this he felt a lump rise in his throat as he realized that it wasn't over, and wouldn't be for a long time. Helping Ann Randall wouldn't end it for either

Nick or Sally. They were both scarred. How deep, he didn't know. What he did know was that here was a little girl who had been robbed of the normal childhood fun of a sleepover.

The fear of not being allowed back home was real to Sally. How long would it last? Nick thought. A week? A month? A year or longer? He didn't have the answers. All he knew was that it wasn't right.

"Mr. Roanik?" Ann tore into his thoughts. "Are you there? Will you be a witness to Danny's behavior?"

Nick cleared his throat and looked at the journal again. "Ms. Randall, when we first met we tried to tell you that Danny had problems. That he needed help. But you refused to listen. You hid behind your stereotypes and cookie cutter analysis," Nick told her calmly. "If you had listened to us then, and got him the help he needed, none of us would be in this position. Not you, not me, and certainly not my wife. The only thing that I can tell you now Ms. Randall is, what goes around, comes around."

Then Nick hung up the phone.

EPILOGUE

In the end Nick did end up helping Ann. Not out of compassion for her though. In the month he had left before his court date Nick did some research. He looked into the entries in Danny's journal and discovered that the Mr. Farly mentioned was the same one who Nick had done a story on a while back involving a high school teacher involved in child pornography. Nick looked into his whereabouts since then and found that the disgraced teacher had moved to Iowa to start over. The record, however, followed him and he wasn't able to recover. Nick found out that just five months earlier Mr. Arnold Farly had hanged himself in his garage.

The boy with the marijuana, Eddie Jenkins, was still in the juvenile correctional facility where Nick was told by the supervisor that he had been jumped by five other inmates and beaten so badly that he would be disfigured for life and that he sustained mild brain damage.

Another entry in the journal, also involving D.S.S., tore a boy away from his mother under allegations of sexual abuse. This one turned out better than the others in that the family was eventually reunited but both mother and son are involved in intense therapy.

All of this seriously disturbed Nick. How could one human being carelessly destroy so many lives and not give a damn? Yes, in the end, Nick did turn the journal over to the judge in court. It was enough to get Danny sent to a psychiatric hospital for evaluation and observation.

Did Nick turn it in to get his case dismissed? Or Ann Randall's? Even though that's what happened, no, that wasn't the reason.

Did he do it because of what had happened to the people whose lives were destroyed? In part, yes. He also turned in the journal in part so that Danny would get the help he desperately needed, out of respect for Pam.

If you're asking yourself what was the kicker, the above it all reason for Nick to change his mind, it was what he found written on the last page of the journal.

REMIND JANE HOW MUCH SHE LOVES ME

1. GET GUN

ACKNOWLEDGMENT

I dedicate this book to my beautiful wife Penny. I can not thank her enough for putting up with my mood swings while reliving certain events as I wrote about them. She knew that writing this book was my therapy and supported me through it all. Thank you, baby, I love you.

Special Thanks

I would like to take a moment to thank my friend and fellow writer, Chisto, who patiently, at least to my face, helped me out enormously throughout the publishing part of this project. He not only put up with my Flintstone era knowledge of the Internet, but also helped me regain the passion I've always had for writing. Please check out his book, Committed.

From the person he calls, "The most paranoid non pot smoker he knows", thank you for your patience, (not my strong suit), and help. Mick.

What Goes Around   by Mick Woodhall

www.ingramcontent.com/pod-product-compliance
Lightning Source LLC
Chambersburg PA
CBHW030530030726
47495CB00004B/931